GUARDIANS

GARGOYLES DEN BOOK ONE

Enjoy!

[signature]

Lisa Barry

Witching Hour Publishing Inc.

Copyright © 2013 by Lisa Barry

Witching Hour Publishing, Inc.

ISBN-10: 1943121087
ISBN-13: 978-1-943121-08-3

Editor: Courtenay Dodds www.CourtenayDodds.com

To My Love

You always knew the day would come,
never had a doubt, and that helped me
believe it too. Thank you.

Acknowledgments

I don't know about the rest of you, but I love to read acknowledgment pages. There is something very special about the help and love that an author receives while writing a book, sometimes from the most surprising sources. It makes my heart pitter-patter.

There is so much activity that goes into the completion and release of a book and so many people that helped bring this one to fruition, I hope that I do not forget anyone.

My writers group, the Ink Slingers Guild, has been an encouraging kick in the arse every fortnight. The meetings are always inspiring and a lot of fun too.

My test readers. Rhiannon, who read the first draft and listened through many more, loving the characters right there with me and often helping me choose one of many paths for each of them. Rhi, you are my writer kin. Lucia (my self-proclaimed biggest fan), Erica, Melanie, Belinda, Keri, Erika: your time, care and encouragement were a strong support on those days when I could have easily closed shop.

My editor, Courtenay Dodds. You are an editing Goddess and an unbelievably awesome friend. Cheers to the next one and next one and...

My kidlets. My hubby. You are the best.

Thank you!

Chapter 1

Driving with only some regard to the traffic laws, Sloane Jacobs swallowed hard. Being forced to attend a family wedding had that affect.

Weddings equaled lots of people, which Sloane avoided like a dark alley. She should be happy, excited even. Her cousin Marla was getting married. Except Sloane knew it wouldn't last. She had met Paul a few times. His red and yellow hue told her clearly; he was up to no good.

Sloane cringed at the pomp and circumstance of it all. That and the thought of the people who would be there. They looked at her like she was a nut bag just waiting to be put into a strait jacket. She had long ago stopped telling anyone, especially family, what reality meant to her.

She had also given up on love. Or companionship. Or whatever. She was much too busy keeping herself alienated. Of course, it didn't help that she could see what everyone was feeling. It definitely didn't make date night very intriguing.

After parking, Sloane clicked the trunk

button on her key remote as she started toward the back of her car.

Stopping briefly, she couldn't help but admire the garden of the Knox Center. The statues, the flowers and the fountains gave that earthy, romantic feeling that a wedding should have. Sighing, she pulled the trunk up and found herself looking straight into a pair of dark eyes.

Sloane sucked in a breath and took a step back. Before her heart had a chance to go into overdrive, it strangely calmed and then soothed into a steady rhythm. A set of hands appeared and pulled the eyes, along with a face and torso, to a sitting position in her trunk. The eyes were quickly joined by a smile and Sloane found herself frowning and puzzling over the cheerful teenage boy sitting casually in her trunk.

"Hello, Gray Boy." The words slipped from her mouth before she had a chance to think. The boy's smile only broadened.

"Hello, ma'am. Thank you for the ride. I was hoping you weren't going very far."

Sloane raised an eyebrow at him as she looked him over. He had dark caramel skin that made his teeth look extra white when he smiled, which thus far was a frequent occurrence. He looked Asian to Sloane; slightly sloped eyes, strong cheek bones, thin with lean muscles. A light gray hue surrounded him.

"Is there a good reason, by chance, that you're in my trunk?" she asked, feeling quite calm. If you had asked her just an hour ago what she would do if she found a strange teenager in her trunk she was quite certain it wouldn't be to have a friendly chat and yet, she felt so peaceful. Those with gray hues tended to have that effect on her. Not that she'd seen many or had any clue as to why they lacked any color. She had started calling them *Gray Ones* for lack of a better word and they seemed to be far and few between.

"Actually yes, I do have a good reason if you count getting smashed in the face, shoved in a trunk and then driven to..." the boy, still smiling, looked around before continuing, "the Knox Center."

"You don't look like you just got beat up," Sloane commented as she watched him pull up his long legs and make his way out of the trunk. He made a face that told her he was blushing even if his skin didn't show it.

"I don't bruise easily," the boy said as he stretched out in front of her, then stood straight. He was just a couple of inches shy of her own six-foot frame.

"Hmmm," Sloane answered as she walked past him and looked into her trunk. "I hope they have an emergency iron around here 'cause this dress is going to need one." She pulled out the apricot orange dress and made a face at the thought of having to wear it.

"Sorry about that," the boy said when he saw the look ripple over her face.

"No biggie, uh..."

"Keppin at your service, ma'am."

"No biggie, Keppin. I've got to attend a wedding and all so we'll have to chat some other time. Are you going to be all right?" Sloane closed her trunk and turned to him as she wondered when she had left her trunk open.

"Oh, I'm fine. Thanks again for the 'ride'." His hands made air quotes before he took a cell phone from his pocket and bowed his head slightly, turning to leave. He looked back abruptly and met eyes that hadn't left him.

"Do you see colors in everyone or just me?" he asked. Sloane studied him for a moment before taking a chance.

"I see colors in all people and some animals too. Gray's not very common," she said. Keppin flashed a smile and then turned sober.

"I have someone you should meet," he said. He looked like a boy who had grown up just a little bit too fast. The idea of finding someone who understood the hues was both frightening and inspiring. Curiosity got the better of her. Sloane nodded. Rummaging in her purse for a moment she came up with a pen and an old gas receipt. She wrote her name and number on it and handed it to him. Keppin shoved the paper into his pocket while Sloane stood awkwardly wondering just how much of a bad idea this was.

"Talk to you later then," he said as he started off toward the street. Sloane watched him until her phone startled her.

"I'm coming, I'm coming," she said as she answered it and watched Keppin cross the main road and head down another street. She hung up and pulled her gaze from him. Pausing only to pop a Vitamin B Complex to ease the mental pain she knew was coming, Sloane grabbed the beer the wedding party had asked her to pick up on the way. *That* was when she had popped her trunk, before going into the store. She had intended to put the beer in there but when she came out, she had already forgotten and put it onto the passenger seat floor. At least he hadn't been in the trunk long. Frowning, she turned and headed into the Knox Center.

~~*~~

Ah, weddings. At the reception, Sloane kept her sighs to herself as she sat at her assigned table and watched the goings-on. Sloane knew that when people thought of weddings they thought of love, gifts, cake, dancing. Rolling her eyes, Sloane unfortunately knew what people *really* thought about during weddings. She watched Uncle Joe surrounded by a purplish-green pulsing hue while chatting with his daughter's friend. *Gross.* Then she observed someone's pregnant wife surrounded by envy; a deep, dark green as she watched the sexy, lithe girls dance. But then again, there *was* the comforting sunny yellow of the happy couple, even if short lived, and their not quite as sunny yellow parents and a smattering of others just having a light gold good time.

She briefly thought that her mother should be here, but an earlier phone call had let her know that she wasn't feeling well. Sloane didn't believe it. A light throb in the back of her head was just starting to make itself known when one of Marla's brothers, Tanner, asked her to dance.

Sloane had grown up with Marla, her younger brother Tanner and the eldest brother Jack, if irregularly. Sloane's mother wasn't especially fond of her sister's family and, so it was at the occasional family get-togethers that Sloane was exposed to the varieties of child rearing. For years Tanner had trailed Marla and Sloane at these foo-foo gatherings, both entertaining and annoying the young girls. Sloane had often wondered if the boy had a bit of a crush on her.

In her early teens the rumors got out about Sloane's 'unusual mental break-downs'. Tanner was the only one who never seemed to take much stock in the adult murmurs.

His gesture to dance was both pleasing and disturbing. Despite his sunny disposition, he probably felt bad for her. If anyone could see her hue, she knew it would have been slightly pink with a mask of dull brown; mildly embarrassed and definitely resistive. However, it would be rude to say no, so a dance it was.

One large piece of chocolate cake and six beers later, the room was a virtual rainbow flashing by as she swapped out dancing partners with the best of them. She didn't even worry that she was as tall or taller than most of them, didn't worry that her dark brown hair, originally pulled up and out of her face, was now loose and fancy free. And she definitely didn't worry about the creepy geezer watching her with those purple and green swirls. *Ugh*. Wishing she hadn't seen him, the beer suddenly felt solid in her belly. The acid reflux made her stop dancing and hightail it to the bathroom where she made it as far as the trash bin just inside the door. When nothing else would come out she had the pleasure of turning to find two elderly women staring her down. She didn't even have to see the orange hue tinged with black to feel the malice burning from them. *Bitches.* Sloane gave them a nod, rinsed out her mouth and went to sit outside in the garden to sober up for the drive home.

Chapter 2

Despite the early morning, Liam McDougall took a long swig of his Corona. Pillows piled up behind him, he lay on the twin bed, his feet framing the sides of a TV that took up most of the top of the chest of drawers at the bed's foot. A thin sheet covered his manly bits but the rest was open for view and just cooling down. He took another swig, let it swish around his mouth and finally swallowed before grinning perfect white teeth at the TV.

He watched the news as though it were prime time entertainment. The reporter was going on about the oddity of three would-be criminals being charged with attempted breaking and entering. There was a shot of them tied up together in front of a jewelry store. The helpful citizen who had left them there was nowhere to be found and one of the criminals, name withheld, was having a mental break down, blaming a large ferocious monster for their misfortune.

Liam chuckled, running a hand through his unruly red hair. Getting news coverage was unusual for a Guardian, not like anyone knew that he was the helpful citizen. The creatures he normally took care of were supposed to be figments of the human imagination. He was just about to get in a good scratch when his phone went off, the alarm ring that only could mean one thing. He jumped off the bed, the sheet falling to the floor, found his jeans and pulled the phone out.

Sitting on the edge of the bed he read the text. ASSIGNMENT. AIRPORT 1230PM. PURPLE KANGAROO. Liam rolled his blue eyes at the humor and checked the time; he had three hours. Smiling he thought, *finally*. Things were just starting to get boring. Throwing on his jeans and blue tee he searched for his sneakers. Finding one under the bed and the other by the door, he shuffled into them and checked: spectacles, testicles, wallet, watch and phone. Yep, he had everything. He went out the bedroom door, down the hall and crossed the living room heading for the front door.

"Hey, Red. Would you like some coffee?" a sultry voice called from the kitchen.

"I've got to rush. Duty calls," Liam answered, although he would have enjoyed a cup. A moment later a woman came into the living room, her thin blue robe hanging open and her blond hair tangled.

"Work?" she asked disdainfully. He watched her fold her arms under her exposed chest and the small smile that tickled her lips. Liam couldn't resist. He sauntered toward her and stopped just before touching. She looked up at him, smirking with her pretty little lips. Leaning down he kissed each of her cheeks gently, then pushed a stray strand of hair behind her ears.

"I'll see you next time I'm in town," he said as he ran a hand lightly down her exposed chest. He smiled once more and left. She didn't come running after him, which Liam appreciated. He knew he'd never see Tanya...or was it Tara? Either way, he wouldn't see her again.

After a quick stop at his temporary apartment to pack up and shower, he was on his way to the airport. He returned his rental car and then made his way through the airport to the first coffee shop he ran across. He folded his long legs into a booth by the window and sipped coffee while watching the planes coming and going. Someone stopped at his table. He waited before looking.

"Excuse me, sir?" Her voice was strong and syrupy. He turned his head and met her gaze. She was cute. Had he the time...

"Do you have the time?" she asked.

Liam stifled a grin and glanced at his watch. "It's quarter past two." He smiled at her and she looked away, glancing at the entrance.

"Thank you. How are you today?"

"Well, I'm just great except for losing my purple kangaroo. Shame that was."

She smiled at him with nicely shaped full lips. "I know what you mean," she said as she held out an envelope. Liam took it and nodded. She smiled again, and he watched her saunter off before breaking the envelope's seal. He glanced at the ticket, checked the gate number and went to find it.

~~*~~

It was a short flight. Liam pulled his duffel from the overhead compartment and left the plane. It was late afternoon and after sleeping the two hours on the plane he was completely rested. Tampa Airport was easy to navigate, and Liam quickly found himself at baggage claim. As he stood watching the luggage glide by he stretched his legs and arms to loosen up. Stretching at every opportunity was a habit Liam had developed when he was younger. It helped him to stay flexible and ready to shift at any moment.

He felt someone glide up next to him and turned. Not as tall as Liam's six foot plus stature, a stocky man wearing cargo pants and a Quiksilver tee-shirt stood next to him. With spiky blond hair, tanned skin and unusual, golden eyes, he emulated the surfer next door.

"Noah!" Liam smiled. "Good to see you!" They grasped hands and slapped each other's shoulders.

"You too, man," Noah said, his voice soft and low. " I'd prefer it were on better terms, like a vacation or something."

Liam pursed his lips in thought before asking, "That bad, huh?"

Noah nodded. Liam left his hand on Noah's shoulder for just a moment and searched his cat-like eyes. Liam gave a joyless smile. "Well, hopefully I can help."

Liam turned, his black duffel already slung over a shoulder and waved his hand with a flourish.

"Lead the way, my friend," he said. Noah led the way to a pair of blue elevators.

"We have a community den that you can stay at during your visit," Noah said as the elevator doors slid open. Inside was a couple that looked like they had just flown around the earth twice. Liam and Noah stepped in, Noah hit the button for the garage level and they rode in silence.

When they arrived at the garage level, the humidity slapped Liam in the face like a wet towel and he stopped to suck in the heavy air. It allowed him to acclimate almost instantly and he followed Noah to a newer blue jeep.

"Nice ride," Liam commented as he tossed his bag into the rear. "What is it?"

"It's a tricked-out Rubicon."

"Nice, man."

"I love this thing, but I wish I'd never sold my CJ-7. That thing was awesome."

"Oh right, I remember that. That *was* sweet," Liam commented as he climbed into the passenger seat without bumping his head. "But you know me; I like two wheels and a shitload of horsepower."

Noah chuckled and began to navigate through the dark garage. When they hit daylight, they both pulled out sunglasses to hide from the setting sun. Liam paid attention to the signage and surroundings. It wasn't his first visit to the area, but it had been long enough that he needed to adjust himself to his new temporary home.

"When is the briefing?" Liam asked as they left Tampa and started over the Causeway toward Clearwater.

"We were going to wait for one more Special Ops to show up, but he won't be in for another two days. I'll give you the quick rundown while we wait for Brick to show."

Liam brought his head up in surprise. "Brick's coming?"

"Yep."

"You're definitely going to have to fill me in then. Brick doesn't get called in for just anything."

Noah stifled a mirthless laugh. "So I hear. I've never met him, but we need all the help we can get. Special Ops generally deals with information leaks, inhuman interference or rogue Guardians." Liam watched as Noah's face turned grim. "But have you ever had to deal with missing Guardians?"

"What do you mean, missing Guardians?"

"Missing, just vanished. Three in the last four months."

"No shit?" Liam asked incredulously.

Noah flattened his lips and nodded his head. Liam rubbed his face. Guardians were tasked to protect themselves and humans from the scary things. Guardians didn't just disappear. "Are you sure they actually disappeared, didn't just go rogue?" he finally asked.

"That's an interesting question. We've looked

at it, but the question kept coming up...how is it that all three went rogue in such a short time period? It just doesn't make sense. So, after the last report the Guardianship said it was time to send in Special Ops."

Liam grunted an acknowledgment and sat quietly for a few minutes. He watched Tampa Bay go by on either side of them as they headed into the city.

"Who is missing?" he finally asked.

"Caden Lister, Reilly Michaels and Joseph Taylor."

Liam's heart thudded in his chest. "Joseph Taylor, the wild man?"

Noah had just started to slow down for a stop light and glanced over at him with a nod. Liam took a deep breath and willed his heart to calm, his emotions to ebb.

"Any ideas at all on what happened to him?"

"Nothing," Noah answered. "He went to his post as far as anyone knows and never came home."

"And the others?"

"It's the strangest thing. I've been to all their last locations and found little that will help. In one alley there was a spot of dried blood. There was also a syringe under one of the dumpsters, but we don't know if those have anything to do with this. They just vanished."

"Where was Joseph posted?" Liam asked as they headed into downtown Clearwater.

"He was in Dunedin on an interim post watching a little old lady's place, for some reason her lot attracts gremlins, while her normal Guardian was on vacation. I don't know if he even knew on the issue of the post. The Guardianship just loves a mystery."

"I think they do it for our own safety but it sure can be annoying."

"Extremely. So anyway, as far as we know, he left for his post and never came back. He kept his clothes bag in a public bathroom in the middle of a park. It wasn't there when we checked it out."

"Hmmm. And what about you? Do you have a post or are you assigned to this like me?"

"I was posted in St. Pete but they replaced me last night, so I could assist on this assignment." Noah glanced at Liam. "Joseph was my trainer when I arrived. You knew him as well?"

Liam cleared his throat. "We were in training together. He's a good friend. I didn't realize he was posted here."

Chapter 3

After hitting the sheets in the wee hours of the morning, Sloane woke midafternoon curled up in a ball on her bed. Her eyes were partially glued shut, her cheeks felt like she'd just had Botox, not that she would know what *that* was like, and a dull ache was pushing on the back of her skull. She pushed herself up and quickly pulled her hand back from the cold, wet spot on the pillow. Her tears were still wet. A sigh escaped her when her feet hit the ground, heels still on. The urge to cry hit her again but she pushed it away. She had made it through the wedding thanks to the drinks. She was so tired.

Tired of crying, tired of headaches, tired of *hues.* Sloane held back a psychotic break of laughter. She'd been losing it a little too often lately. She had almost gone to see her step-father, a well-known psychiatrist, to ask for help but her sanity had returned just in time. She may be lost and miserable, but she didn't need to add drugged and incoherent to the list.

Wondering again how she had managed to reach twenty-three, Sloane made her way to the bathroom and splashed cold water onto her face.

She looked into her bloodshot eyes and poked at her puffy cheeks. After sticking her tongue out at herself she grabbed some Vitamin B1 from the kitchen cabinet and a bottle of water. It didn't totally keep her little pity parties away, but it helped.

An hour later, the late afternoon sun pouring through the living room window, Sloane found herself with little done to speak of.

The thought of snuggling down with a good book and a cup of coffee brought her to life. Coffee. Coffee cured almost anything and luckily Sloane lived only a block from one of the best coffee shops in town. She checked her purse and was rewarded with the change from the beer she'd stopped to buy yesterday. Checking the stash in her underwear drawer she was rewarded with enough for a new paperback. It was time to indulge.

As she started to shut the front door, Sloane noticed the squirrel standing on the outside of the living room windowsill, looking in. It glanced up and saw her. She swore it was smiling as Sloane met its eyes for a moment and then waved as she usually did. It put a hand on the window and continued to look at her. Sloane shook her head, amused, then shut and locked the door behind her.

As she strolled over to her car she remembered her encounter with Keppin and wondered what he was all about. With her luck he'd lose her number and she'd never see him again. Just wander aimlessly through life wondering why she'd been the one to get stuck seeing the hues. Surely if everyone else had the problem it would be commonly known. *Right?*

Chapter 4

The community den turned out to be a nicely furnished four-bedroom condo on the tenth floor of a barely filled complex. Liam tossed his duffel into his assigned room and was glad to see he would be sleeping in a cozy king size bed. The walls were empty, but everything was modern and well kept. The Guardianship moved the dens frequently to avoid attention but since the building had so few tenants, they might be able to stay put for a while.

The living room and dining area were next to the kitchen and just outside a hallway from the front door. Liam and Noah sat at the dining room table which was strewn with papers, pencils, odds and ends. Noah held up a bag containing a syringe. "This is what we found at Caden's post. It was under a dumpster."

Liam took the bag and inspected it. "You have a safe place to get this tested? See if there's any DNA or blood to indicate one of ours."

"I'll find out."

Liam nodded as Noah handed him another bag. Liam looked at the dried brown specks. "Blood?"

"Yep. It was on the ground at Reilly's hang

out. Not sure if it's relevant or not."

"Better get them both tested. If you direct me to the nearest motorcycle rental and bookstore I'm going to get myself a bike and grab a map. I just need to re-acclimate myself since I was here last. We'll want to get this research done and laid out before Brick arrives and see if it leads to anything."

~~*~~

Liam was pleased with his bike, a sleek and fast Ducati. Joe's Motorcycle Rental had been only two blocks away, so it had taken him no time to walk there and make his selection. Thanks to Noah's easy directions he zipped through Clearwater to the local Barnes and Noble. The moment he walked in the door the burnt smell of coffee invaded his senses and he steered left to Starbucks. All coffee was good as far as Liam was concerned. He brought the coffee over to the map section and found the one he needed. After wandering a bit to find an open chair he finally settled near the fiction books.

Looking over the street names his memory started to rush back in. He knew he had tucked the information away for a day like this. Scanning the map and committing any major roads he wasn't familiar with to memory he was just about to stand when he saw her.

She was perusing the new fiction releases, her deep brown, almond shaped eyes scanning across the books, lightly glossed full lips reading their titles silently. He watched her frown and shake her head periodically, her wavy hair falling delicately on and down her shoulders. She was dressed in a blue tank top and plaid surfer shorts that showed off her beautiful curves and legs that could kill. Liam's heart thudded in his chest. He inhaled a calming breath only to be struck with...her scent. Oh god, her scent. It seeped into every part of his being leaving him with a heady feeling of having just finished a fine whiskey.

Not knowing if he should curse or bless his innate amplified senses, Liam calmed himself like he would before countering an attack; something he experienced fairly regularly on his job, but not usually in a quiet book store.

He watched as she picked up a book and read the back. The pleasant look of contemplation on her face as she read made Liam smile. She chose and headed to the front of the store.

Liam stood quickly and followed her, in the stealthy pursuit of a prize way. Watching from behind a best sellers display as she paid for her book, he puzzled over her as she seemed to look everywhere except at the teller. He glanced at the teller but couldn't see anything unusual. His conquest, *Legs,* slid her purchase off the counter and practically ran to the door. He followed slowly and watched her climb into an older model sports car. Waiting until he saw the direction she pulled out of the parking lot he sprinted to his bike, gunned it and followed. He smiled to himself as he played her road game and weaved in and out of traffic behind her. The thought of a woman who could actually drive filled him with pride.

She pulled into an alley behind a coffee shop, conveniently close to his den he noted, so he pulled over to street parking and waited. Knowing he would be spotted in the alley he was just about to head down on foot when she came around the corner carrying the bag from the book store and went into the coffee shop.

Chapter 5

Café Bliss was one of those off the beaten path coffee shops that had been there forever but most of the locals don't even know about it. Modernly furnished with art deco pictures and bright colors accenting the warm beiges and black, Sloane loved it because it was peaceful. Not too many people hung around, usually getting their coffee and moving on. The best chair was a large brown semi-recliner that was usually available. She sank into it and opened the book in her lap.

Sloane was staring absently at the door when he came in. Her heart fluttered as she took in a short, quick breath and glanced away, afraid she might meet his eye. Only seconds passed before she found him again; her eyes following him to the counter. She couldn't remember ever having *this* reaction to a man. The feeling was as real as a spike of double shot espresso hitting the blood stream and it was happening in her own stomping ground. She heard him place his order, his voice deep and silky. Was a silky voice even possible? *Caramel macchiato* he had said.

She watched him stand at the counter patiently; not like he had any other choice. Café

Bliss ground the coffee and made it there for you nice and fresh. Sometimes you had to wait for a good thing. She saw that his chocolate brown tee shirt was not too tight and not too loose. She could tell that he worked out or was one of those lucky bastards who magically stayed in shape. She couldn't think of anyone that wouldn't mind laying a hand on one of his arms or... Sloane sighed. She realized she was smiling stupidly at him and jerked her arm out in surprise almost knocking her coffee off the side table. Quickly laying her eyes back on her book where she had been trying to get past the first page it wasn't but a moment before her eyes trailed off again. She didn't think he had noticed, he was looking at a newspaper that someone had left on the counter.

The one thing that stood out like a nighttime explosion was his hair. Short in the back and longer on the top it apparently had a mind of its own. It was about as helter-skelter as hair can get and it was a vibrant red. Perfect cream-colored skin, chiseled cheeks and jawbones like stone, Sloane watched as he gazed at the treaties in the glass case. And his eyes; blue, a beautiful burning blue. She felt the heart flutters start up again.

Sloane waited patiently for him to get his drink and leave. She stared at her book, trying to look engrossed, glancing up every two seconds. She had stupidly left the house without any regard to how she might look. Her wavy, dark brown hair fell messily past her shoulders, well that was actually normal, and her face, void of make-up save a little gloss to avoid dry lips, probably looked like she had only slept half the night, which would be true. She sighed again as she gave up, packed away her book and stood. Grabbing her purse and bag, she cast a last look at Red and froze.

He was not just looking at her, oh god no, but standing with his arms crossed in front of him and outright staring at her. Three shades of red hit her with such force she worried steam might actually start pouring from her skin. Sloane glanced behind her but, being in the corner, it was a wasted move. There was no possible way he was looking at someone else. She glanced back at him and found he had cocked his head and had a half smile on his lips.

Slamming her sunglasses onto her face Sloane bolted straight past him and for the door without a glance behind her. She pushed her way to the outside, to normal people who didn't stop her heart, nice, normal people who made her see things she didn't want to, made her cry and hurt inside. She didn't stop until she was around the corner and heading toward her apartment, then she felt calm again. Or at least calmer. No man could have her, she just wasn't made right.

A thought that had been festering in the back of her mind finally came to the surface. Sloane stopped dead in the alley, staring ahead at nothing. She was always calm, actually calmed, by them, always. Until now.

He was a Gray One.

Chapter 6

Liam stood on the rooftop of the coffee house, wings folded back, coffee in hand and watched Legs make her way down the alley toward a small but quaint duplex entrance. The wind tossed his red hair around like a rag doll and he shielded his eyes from it. He took in a deep breath, letting the scent of her violet perfume, and something else that was just her, fill a void he hadn't known was there. It filled his senses as completely as the blood pounding through his veins.

He frowned as she stopped mid stride and stood unmoving, her coffee halfway to her lips. Liam quickly stepped back from the edge of the roof concerned that she might look up and see him standing there, partially changed. No one ever looks up he thought as curiosity got the better of him. He leaned back over the edge.

He watched her slowly lower her coffee as she stared straight ahead. Then, as though a switch had been flipped, her stride started up again and he watched her disappear behind the duplex door. Liam backed up and leaned on the edge of an air conditioner. Staring out at the clear, blue sky he had to put effort into smoothing out the rush of emotion that had his blood pumping. His endocrine system was working overtime and his nerves felt like they were trying to jump out of his skin. He started as he realized an earlier thought. *Conquest.*

Years, he thought. It had been years since his control had gone wayward like this. Crushing emotion into a pocket in the back of his mind he closed his eyes and forced a calm. He took a swig of coffee and consciously followed it; tasting it on his tongue, feeling the warmth down his throat, through his esophagus and into his stomach where acids started breaking it down.

Then he focused. On Joseph. On the missing Guardians. The strange new feelings melted back into their den and the hard logical side became solid again. Jumping down from the rooftop his stride took him away from her door as he headed toward his bike. He didn't even have to fight the urge to turn back.

Not much at least.

Chapter 7

Sloane closed the door behind her and leaned against it. As she let her heart settle a bit she wondered why this one had affected her so differently from the other Gray Ones she'd seen. And what sets them apart from normal people?

From an early age Sloane had learned not to talk about what she saw. The look of concern and sometimes terror that she saw in her mother's face was enough to quiet her comments and observations. Over time she had started to understand most of the colors. Each individual was different. There were similar hues, as she liked to call them, but she could see the subtle differences. She could sometimes read a person's chronic personality, but it was their current mood that was the easiest.

The Gray Ones were the ones she couldn't read. It was like they had no emotion, or were blocked from her somehow, and they always made her feel calm. She had thought that it should be the opposite, that knowing what people were feeling would be better than not, but it didn't work that way. Something about not knowing, about having to guess made her feel more normal and that was comforting.

Based on her meeting with Keppin, the Gray Ones might even know what this hue thing was. Hell, maybe they think it's a blessing. She'd always thought of it as a curse, even though it had saved her from heartbreak in relationships and friends many times. Maybe she should look at it as a friend. Then she remembered that she only had one friend to speak of and went back to it being a curse.

Sloane suddenly desperately hoped that Keppin would get back to her. Have her meet someone or a group that could help her, someone who could shed some light on this thing she'd carried alone her entire life. Would someone be able to help her find purpose?

Sloane was knocked out of her thoughts when the cell phone she'd left on the coffee table sung out at her. She smiled and picked it up.

"What up, girl?"

"Sloane! Where have you been? I've called four times!" Nia's velvety voice was an octave higher than normal.

"I'm fine. Geez. I went to buy a book and get a coffee."

"You do know that a cell phone is also known as *mobile* phone, don't you?"

"Yes, Nia. Or should I call you mother?" Sloane laughed at her one friend. "I thought you were off camping or whatever it is you do on the weekends and never invite me."

Nia sighed, and Sloane realized she had overstepped. Nia never told her what she was up to and Sloane had learned to keep her mouth shut about it, only slipping sometimes.

"Never mind," Sloane said. "What's so urgent?"

"Nothing really. I guess I am mothering. I just called to chat and was alarmed when you kept not answering."

"Well, I really am fine. You want to come over and watch a movie or something?" Sloane asked.

"I'd love to! Be over in a few." Nia hung up.

Sloane shook her head. It was kind of nice having at least one person who gave a shit what happened to you. The only time her mom called was if she was late for their weekly Sunday dinner.

Nia always had a soft, white hue, her emotions a perfect tranquil fusion. It was one of the main reasons Sloane had ended up befriending her, that and Nia's persistence, and Sloane was thankful for it. It had started with a chance meeting in the Teacher's Lounge where Sloane had taken a rare moment from driving her school bus to refill her coffee cup.

When she had walked into the room Nia's tall, lithe figure, complete with perfectly fitted pink and white designer suit, was on hands and knees. Her long white-blond hair draped on the floor as she peered beneath the wheeled coffee cabinet. Sloane had watched as Nia stuck a long arm beneath it and pulled back with a satisfied exclamation.

Leaning against one of the dull green lounge chairs, Sloane had watched in amusement as Nia pulled herself up, a broad smile on her face, her cool silvery eyes sparkling.

"If I didn't know better I'd think you found a good man under there," Sloane commented.

Nia made a disgruntled noise but kept smiling. She held out her hand where a silver heart shaped earring lay.

"I lost it the other day and finally decided to search the damn place."

Sloane had smiled and gone to the counter for coffee, prepping up to ignore her. Nia had leaned an elbow on the counter while she filled her cup at the urn.

"We meet at last," she'd said. Sloane's surprise must have shown on her face.

"I've seen you around," Nia continued. "You never talk to anybody, always keeping your head to the ground," she lifted her hands and pointed at herself as she spoke, "I'm a bit more social. You need a friend and I'm it."

Sloane laughed aloud as she thought about the look that must have crossed her face. She had resisted that reach for friendship for weeks, but Nia had persisted and finally gotten her to agree to go out for coffee. Nia's easy manner and outlook on life, coupled with the serenity of her soft hue, had finally solidified their friendship. Sloane realized much later that Nia had needed a friend as much as she had, so despite their wide differences they filled a void for each other. It also helped Sloane to know that Nia hid something, a deep dark something. Since Sloane did too, it only seemed fair.

Hearing a knock at the door, Sloane opened it

to face a smiling Nia. Dressed to the hilt in a silver tee, powder blue work-out pants and designer sneakers, Nia held out a bag of fresh donuts.

"Treaties!" she hollered as she slid into the apartment. Sloane laughed as they plopped down on the loveseat.

"Oh my God! Did you see what Kevin was wearing on the last day of school? No, of course you didn't!" Nia rolled her eyes at Sloane. "You have got to start looking around, girl. He wore a complete three-piece suit, vest and all! He was sweating so profusely in this heat. It was awful! I think he did it because he's sweet on Ms. Judy. She was chatting it up with him during break! It was awesome!"

Sloane laughed again. Nia was the part-time music teacher for grades 1-3. Also single, how she could possibly afford the threads she wore Sloane had no idea, but that was just another mystery of Nia. Next to her love of music, Nia found other people's love lives fascinating, almost to a fault. Like Sloane, she seemed to avoid her own love life like the plague.

Biting into a donut Sloane tossed a movie at her. Nia glanced at the cover. *Ever After.*

"Again? Don't you have anything new?"

Sloane shook her head and smiled as she chewed. Nia slapped her knee.

"We are so going to the theatre. My treat!"

Chapter 8

Andy watched the concrete rush toward him. As he fell he could hear the counselor call his name, as if that would suddenly revert gravity. He winced as a rock sliced into his knee and then the rest of his body hit the black top with a thud.

He was barely down when the basketball team surrounded him, clucking like females. He had to fight not to laugh. His hands went to his knee, protecting it from further battering when the counselor forced his way through the crowd of boys.

"Haven't had a good accident lately, huh, Andy?" Counselor Sam said. Andy wondered if he meant something more as he inspected the bloody wound.

"Well, you'll live this time," Sam commented as he helped Andy off the blacktop and then resumed the game.

Andy sat to the side of the blacktop with three of the reserve players. He leaned back into the fence and watched the basketball game. Less than a year ago Andy had started to notice odd changes in himself. Not only did the pain tolerance that he was used to increase significantly but his ability to heal changed. It was fast and not just a little fast either. A small cut or scratch would be gone so fast he wouldn't have a chance to show anyone. A larger cut, like the one he'd just gotten, would take maybe ten minutes to heal. He hadn't broken anything yet, although he'd come close, so he didn't know what to anticipate there.

Every now and then Andy would purposely fall or do something to hurt himself to see what would happen. It always healed up and Andy wondered if Sam was catching on.

There were other changes. He could see well in the dark, almost as well as daytime, and he didn't feel extreme cold or hot. He hadn't had the opportunity to do a lot of testing, but he was pretty sure his speed and agility had increased, a lot. When he was playing ball, he had to miss the hoop or screw up on purpose. He'd seen what happened to kids that had unusual or spectacular smarts or abilities. Drugs. The kind that legally fry your mind.

He had no idea who he could trust. The thought made his heart twitch as his parents came to mind. They would know; he was sure of it. Only they weren't here. *Here* was in an orphanage awaiting adoption or legal age. Being sixteen, he was certain that hitting eighteen was the more likely thing to happen. He had enough problems without trying to fit in with a family now.

The counselor, being referee, bounced around the black top whistling periodically or clapping someone on the back for a job well done. Andy glanced down at his knee again. Earlier there had been a gash with enough blood to force him out of the game but not enough to cause concern. Now his knee looked like it had murdered someone and forgot to wash away the evidence. Dried blood covered it and only a faint line was visible. He knew even that would be gone soon too. He would have to wear pants for the next few days, he thought.

Normal people took a few days to recover from a gash or scrape, normal people had scars. If things like this hadn't happened before he might've been freaked but since they had, now he just frowned and continued watching the game. It finally ended and everyone packed up to head back to the orphanage for dinner, a fifteen-minute walk away.

Sam leaned down to inspect Andy's knee. He frowned and looked at Andy, who just shrugged.

"Seems to be healing up just fine," Sam commented as he held out a helping hand.

"Yes sir," Andy said as he took the proffered hand, even though he didn't need the help.

The nine boys and counselor left the public courts and crossed 1st Street to an alley that led between a rundown drug store and beauty supply shop that had also seen better days. Taking the alley, although it was pretty rank, cut out at least five minutes, possibly more, from their walk back to the orphanage.

Andy had never been able to think of the orphanage as home. He had arrived when he was eight, already knowing what a real home and parents were like. He knew what he was missing, and he *was* missing. The bummer was that if his mom and dad had any relations, no one, including Andy had any idea who they were. So, he had ended up here in the Tampa Bay area, alone. That was half his life ago. Many kids had come and gone, but a few, like him, seemed to have stuck around for the long haul.

"You should turn yourself in to some science experiment group who can test you to find out how it is you heal so damn fast," Eric said quietly, his tone jealous. They were at the back of the group heading to the end of the alley.

If Andy had to call someone a close friend, he wouldn't but if he had to, Eric would have to be it. Eric had arrived at the orphanage two years before Andy. He had been assigned Andy's 'buddy' and had helped him groove in. Eric had seen Andy cry his first few days there and had given him space when he needed it. He was a good person.

"I'm not interested in being drugged, sliced and diced but thanks for the tip," Andy replied with a frown. He sure didn't want to be noticed. He'd seen way too many movies showcasing people with special abilities or whatever and they usually ended up dead. He'd seen kids at the orphanage excel at something only to be prescribed some drug to 'help' them and he'd watched their light fade. His parents had warned him about those drugs and he was going to keep in the shadows. He thought he had better start being smarter about his experiments in public, like stop doing them.

"Attention!" Sam called. That was his code for: 'Get into double lines, face forward and be quiet.' There was always a reason for it; crossing a busy road, settle everyone down, showing off for the government people who cruised through the building periodically. From where Andy stood whatever had brought it on was yet to be seen.

He heard the odd chanting as soon as everyone had finally gone quiet. Apparently, another skill he had gained was enhanced hearing. As he and Eric trod along behind the others, Eric finally heard it too. He gave Andy a quizzical glance. Andy raised his shoulders and shook his head.

The boys came to a stop at the end of the alley and waited for traffic to calm. That left Andy and Eric right next to the mysterious chanter, who hadn't stopped despite the company.

The derelict was wearing a dirty green tee, faded slacks, old sneakers and fingerless gloves. Andy had seen gloves like that in movies and wondered what on earth they were good for. The bum's hair and beard were long and scraggly, and Andy glanced over just in time to see Eric's nose wrinkle in distaste.

Andy turned back to the bum with detached interest. He never could figure out why anyone would want to live out on the streets. The bum must have felt the attention and glanced up. Meeting Andy's eyes, he stopped chanting abruptly.

"You!" he growled, baring yellowed and black teeth. Andy felt his heart speed up and raised a questioning eyebrow but didn't back away. Eric inhaled loudly in surprise. The look of fear in the bum's face was so profound that Andy held out his hand to try to calm him. He felt an odd tingle in his skin, a bit like goose bumps, as he reached out.

"Yer one of 'em! God protect me!" the guy whispered before taking off toward the opposite end of the alley. Andy stared after him, stunned. He watched until the bum rounded the corner of the alley and was out of sight. Andy's heartbeat started to return to normal and he turned to look at Eric.

Eric was staring in disbelief, not at the alley exit but at Andy. In his face was surprise and, Andy realized, fear.

"What?" Andy asked defensively. Eric just gave his head a slight shake as though he couldn't speak. Before Andy could ask more, Sam was beside them.

"What just happened?" Sam asked in full on defense mode. The other boys had fallen out of file and were talking or horsing around.

"That guy looked at me, said 'you are one of them' and then ran screaming," Andy told him honestly, puzzled at the incident. Sam laughed.

"You probably just scared him," Sam said with his usual you'll-suddenly-feel-better pat on the back.

"Sure," Andy said, "That's probably it." He

glanced over at Eric whose tongue was stilled tied and who studiously inspected his fingernails.

As they moved on, Andy glanced down the now empty alley and wished he had parents.

Chapter 9

"I think I may have another one for you, sir."

"What makes you think that?"

"He's different, Doctor J. He...um...heals himself."

"Last I checked that was something we all do naturally, Sam." The name rolled off the man's tongue like it tasted bad.

"Yes, sir. I know, sir. But this one heals faster than normal. In minutes instead of days."

"Hmm. The last one you sent was normal. You don't want to know what happened to him." Doctor J paused and chuckled. "But that one you sent a couple of years ago...she was valuable. Keep an eye on your boy and see if you notice anything else. Then call me."

"Yes, sir. I will."

Doctor J dropped the phone into his pocket and nodded to his assistant who promptly took his hand off the specimen's mouth, stepping back.

"Now Joseph," he said, "Let's see if 750 volts loosens your tongue."

Chapter 10

Sloane sat at the dining room table and watched her mother hand wash the dishes from dinner. She had long since lost the argument to share the chore and ended up staring intently at the back of her mother's head. A soft yellow glow had always surrounded her mother until the day her father didn't come home. Sloane had been eight. It had been the hardest year they'd ever had. No one knew where he'd gone, he had just disappeared.

Her mother's hue had gone back and forth between yellow and blue-green for years, but it was still her; Sloane's mom and friend. A few years ago her hue had turned a pale bilious green. She had simply changed. Overnight. She'd not been the same since. The once caring and smiling lady became almost a stranger.

Not long after, Sloane met her soon to be stepfather, Reagan. No matter what mood was on the outside, his hue rarely changed from its soft yellow and green veined glow. Sloane didn't care for him, but her mom only seemed happy around him, so Sloane kept it to herself. Living on her own now, Reagan still gave her the creeps though she couldn't put her finger on why. He was a psychiatrist and ran a mental health institute as well as taught a class at the local college. Even after he married her mother he barely gave Sloane any attention and she often wondered if that was any indication as to how he treated his patients. Her thoughts were interrupted by her mother's voice.

"Have you given any more thought to Gio?"

"Ugh. Mom, do we really have to go there? I don't know why it's such a big deal to you. I would think you'd be happy that I'm holding out for the guy that makes my heart flip and turns my nerves to fire. Gio ain't it." Sloane's heart did a flip-flop at the thought of a certain redhead.

"How do you even know that if you don't give the boy a chance?"

"First he's not a boy. He's twenty-four and soon to be graduating in Reagan's favorite subject. Second there's no spark. No goosebumps. No interest. And that's after he's been over for dinner at least five times in the last couple of months when I happen to be here. Why don't we talk about why you stay home all day waiting to do Reagan's beck and call, forgetting that you have your own life and have an amazing talent as a painter?" Sloane regretted the words the moment they left her mouth. They couldn't hang out together anymore without her mother trying to push Gio on her and her trying to get her mom back to her passion. Or what had once been her passion.

Clara Johnson stared at her daughter for a moment. A confused look crossed briefly over her face before she smiled.

"Would you like some pie? I made it fresh this morning. Reagan does love a fresh blueberry pie." Sloane rolled her eyes. Another twilight zone moment. She shook her head.

"No thanks, Mom. I'm not actually fond of pie. You could warm it up so that you and Reagan can enjoy it when he returns from the store."

"Oh, that's a lovely idea. I'll put on the tea too. He should be back soon."

Reagan had run out after dinner to pick up some new book he had ordered. He said it would give her *quality* time with her mother.

"Actually Mom, I have to go. You can get everything ready for Reagan, I have a couple of errands to run before I get home and I want to get a good night sleep."

"Oh, I understand, honey. It's very important to be well rested." As Sloane stood her mother finished drying her hands on the sunflower patterned dishtowel and turned to face her. Sloane leaned in and squeezed her close.

"I love you, Mom."

"You're a good girl, Sloane," her mother said dreamily, her hug light and informal. Sloane let go and her mother's arms dropped automatically to her sides and the social smile turned on.

"Oh, I almost forgot, dear!" Her mother rushed to the freezer. "Reagan was sure you would want your special smoothie."

Smoothie in hand, Sloane left the cookie cutter house nestled in one of the who's-who of Clearwater neighborhoods and climbed into her car. Every single week since Reagan had come into her life he made her the smoothie. Supposedly it was protein and mineral rich and would keep her healthy. Sloane had originally thought it was to appease her mother's constant concern for her health but now she wondered. She normally drank it quickly, the strange bitter flavor made it unpleasant, but this time she just tucked it into the cup holder.

Staring at her childhood home, she remembered fighting tears every time she left; now she couldn't leave fast enough. Her heart squeezed painfully. She missed her mom. Before she could contemplate the past any further, her phone rang out a funky techno beat. Her sadness vanished as she stared at the unknown number. Instinct brought her thumb to the ignore button and then she remembered.

"Yes?" she answered dryly.

"Sloane?" the voice queried in a familiar tone, seeing as how she had relived their one and only conversation a hundred times in her head.

"The one and only." And so true.

"It's Keppin. You know, from your trunk? They're meeting tonight. It's kinda secret, so meet me where we met before and I'll take you there."

Sloane was silent. A strange teenager wanted her to meet him in a dark parking lot. She would be nuts to do something so stupid.

"Sure. Be about fifteen minutes," she answered and ended the call. A slim baby-blue Cadillac pulled into the driveway next to her. She revved the engine and waved at Reagan as she backed out of the driveway. He smiled and waved as he headed toward the house. A chill went down her spine when she saw her mother open the door for him, grinning like a sheep before slaughter. Death would probably be more pleasant than another dinner in that house.

Sloane headed to her secret rendezvous. Flipping on her fuzz buster she hit the gas pedal.

Chapter 11

"You flickered!" Eric whispered intensely.

"What?" Andy's face screwed up as though he had bitten into a lemon. "What are you talking about? What the heck is a flicker?"

"You...you...changed for a second. Into...uh...a shadow sort of." Eric was on his bed in the corner with his legs pulled up to his chin. Andy had finally gotten him alone after dinner and now he was talking mumbo jumbo.

"A shadow?" Andy repeated frustrated, as he sat on his twin bed across the small room from Eric.

"Yeah," Eric whispered again.

"Okay, man. I don't know what's happening, but you have got to relax. I'm still me." Eric nodded at him but didn't relax. Andy rubbed his face and tried to clear his mind. So he had odd special abilities and now Eric's trying to tell him he can turn in to a shadow? *WTF?* he thought.

"Eric?" Andy looked at his friend who hesitantly looked back. "Eric, man. Come on. You've got to stop looking at me like I've grown horns."

"You reminded me of a vampire," Eric said quietly. Andy sighed and lay back on his bed.

"No, there's another explanation. That I am sure of. I love garlic, I'm wearing a silver chain and the only thing that's bitten me lately is a mosquito and no, I am not having any wild cravings for blood."

Eric finally smiled and relaxed slightly.

"I need you to keep this quiet, Eric. I've no idea what's happening but I really don't want to be a science project, okay?"

"Okay, man. Okay." Eric nodded and smiled. "Sorry about that. It was pretty freaky."

"I wish I could've seen it."

Chapter 12

Leaving the windows down and the stereo cranked up, Sloane watched the road while relishing the wind whipping through her hair. It was sometimes the small things that gave her a brief appreciation of life, simple and free. As she zipped by yet another car, the music faded into the background as she wondered yet again if life was worth living for, such as it was. Forever an outcast if for no other reason than her inability to handle the hues.

The answers were not breaking down her door Sloane thought bitterly. With no other options in view, she pulled into the parking lot.

Keppin was exactly where she had parked at their last encounter. He was dressed all in black and looked a little bit on the apprehensive side. Sloane rolled down her window.

"Why do I get the idea that this is not a good idea?"

"No, no. It'll be fine," Keppin said, putting on a sloppy air of certainty. Sloane didn't have to see his colors to know he was nervous about something. He slid into her passenger seat and looked around.

"Cool car. You know how to drive it?" he

challenged. Sloane's look raised his brows and he directed her back downtown. Not long into the drive he put on his seat belt. If there was one thing Sloane enjoyed it was driving. Fast.

A little while later he had her pull the car into a bank parking lot. When they were standing on the sidewalk Keppin took out a camouflage-decorated bandanna.

"You must be kidding me," Sloane said stepping away.

"It's the only way. You can't know where we're going." Sloane got the distinct idea that her welcoming crew didn't know she was coming. *Desperation makes people do silly and dangerous things.* Yeah, she was desperate.

"Fine." It came out angrier than she felt. Keppin covered her eyes and the already dark street vanished to blackness. She didn't remember bandannas working this well when she was a kid. Keppin took her elbow and started walking. Periodically he warned her of steps up or down. After a few minutes of slow moving they finally stopped. Sloane heard the snick of elevator doors and he guided her inside. It was a longer ride than she expected. When it finally stopped he guided her along for only a moment before she heard him knock on a solid door. It was funny, she thought, that she would be able to tell a solid door from a hollow one, but it really did have a distinctive sound. She felt the air change when the door opened.

"Watcha got there, Kep?" a soft female voice asked.

"Someone to meet the boss," Keppin answered. Sloane thought his voice sounded just a little shaky.

"I see," the voice said. It sounded amused. Keppin tugged her elbow and guided her along for several feet before bringing her to a wall where she leaned back, the heavy door distantly clicked shut.

"Keppin," a male voice stated, it was deep and level and somehow familiar. The authority in it was unmistakable. Sloane felt a flicker of annoyance as she tried to place it. She felt Keppin, standing next to her, straighten up.

"Hello, sir," Keppin said, admiration filling his voice.

"Who do you have there?" the low voice asked.

"Oh, for goodness sake. Why not ask me?" Sloane asserted. She reached up, pulled the bandanna off and suddenly wished she was invisible. Her hand flew to her chest in surprise, "Oh."

Red stood with his arms crossed over his chest, leaning back against a table, and two more men stood on the other side. The far two glanced at each other and left the room. Red looked her over from head to toe, just like he had at the coffee shop. Except that he wasn't smiling this time. At all. Sloane felt the heat come up her chest and neck, infiltrating her face like a bold, red wine. An unhappy mixture of anger and, *was that her hormones? How could they even think about such a thing right now?!*

"Fair enough," Red said. It occurred to Sloane that men as good looking as he was probably just thought of women as conquests; easy to lure in and easy to cast off. He had that arrogance about him. It annoyed her that she was so intrigued.

"Who are you?" he finally asked.

Sloane stuttered, "Well, he thought...he was thinking that maybe..."

"Sir!" Keppin jumped in, "I think she's an Aspie!"

Sloane's head whipped over to stare at Keppin.

"A what?" she said, bewildered. "What the heck is that?"

Keppin looked pleadingly at Red who tilted his head slightly and sighed.

"Two things, Keppin. Listen well. Despite your excellent ability to eavesdrop on your brother, you are not to attend another meeting until you have completed your schooling. Do you understand?" His voice was firm bordering on angry. Sloane realized that there were more people in the apartment than she had originally thought. In the back of the room six people, including the two guys she had seen earlier, were peering around the corner. One of them bore a distinct resemblance to Keppin. All except the one light green hued girl who must have answered the door were Gray One's. She turned back to look at Keppin who was shaking slightly and nodding. Keppin was a nice kid. She scowled at Red. He ignored her and continued to lecture the boy.

"The second thing Keppin, is that if you suspect someone of being an Aspie or otherwise, you are to bring it to your brother's attention immediately and then leave it alone."

"Yes sir." Keppin looked like he just might cry, but she thought he held it together pretty well considering. Red brought his hard gaze back to her. She pushed her chin high and scowled back. *What the heck was his problem?*

"Miss...?" he asked. She stared evil woman daggers at him for a moment before answering.

"*I* am Sloane," she said in the haughtiest manner she could. She saw a flicker of amusement cross his sharp features. Figures that she finally ran into someone who made her blood boil in the good way and he turned out to be a prick. No, the King of Pricks.

"So, Sloane," his bossy manner simmered down in a blink and he became a casual inquisitor, "do you see colors when you look at people? Do the colors change depending on how they feel? Do they sometimes tell you what kind of person they are?"

Sloane gaped at him, her heart skipping a few beats while she collected herself. So they *did* know. The real question; was that a good thing or bad thing to them? She glanced at Keppin. He had chilled out since the verbal pounding had stopped and gave her an encouraging smile. She turned back to Red.

"First," she said, "what is your name?"

"Liam." The amused look was back on his face and this time he let it show. Sloane decided not to roll her eyes and continued.

"Well Liam, I feel a bit backed into a corner. I don't know who you people are, what you're up to and if being an 'Aspie' is a good thing or not so I'm sorry if I'm not sure how to answer." She wasn't sorry at all but was feeling mighty snotty. Liam nodded.

"I can see that. I'm not going to explain but I will say that being an Aspie, who by the way *can* do what I mentioned before and sometimes quite a bit more, is only good or bad depending on how the talent is *used*." Sloane felt her guard drop. Emotion welled into her veins like smoke from a burning building. She bowed her head and looked at cement floor.

"Yes, I see them," she said quietly. She never saw or heard him but suddenly he was in front of her. Sloane stepped back and hit the wall. Cool bricks shocked through her clothes as she met his eyes. He looked down at her, all hostility gone, his lips curling into a small, curved smile. She felt her cheeks and arms start to tingle and she quickly moved to inspect his black canvas high tops.

"There's nothing wrong with you, Sloane," he said softly. His deep voice rolled over her like a worn-in blanket. She could feel his eyes on her, waiting. She shuffled her feet some, took in a few deep breaths and finally brought her head up high and looked him straight in the eyes.

"Thank you," she whispered. Sloane was sure she would melt into the concrete when she felt a tear roll down her cheek.

"You're welcome." Liam nodded as he reached up and wiped the tear from her face. Lightning warmth shot down her face and into her fingertips. She froze. Looking into the depths of his eyes she watched them widen for such a fleeting moment that she wondered if she had made it up. He turned away and walked back to the table. He clapped his hands, grabbing everyone's attention, not that he didn't already have it.

"Shows over. Let's get to work. Keppin, please escort the lady home."

"Excuse me, but do you have any tips on how I could learn more about my...*talent*?" Sloane interjected.

"Keppin, explain it to her, will you?"

"Yes, sir!" The pride was back in the kid's voice.

~~*~~

Anger was steaming from Sloane's skin in layers. She felt like a servant being dismissed for the day. Keppin kept his distance as they made their way back to her car. He had forgotten the blindfold and Sloane wasn't about to remind him.

"I think he's cool," Keppin said almost skipping along. "Bummer that I can't get in anymore though." Sloane barely heard him. Her tears had come unbidden with the truth. She wasn't a nut bag. She was normal in someone's definition. The anger fizzled out as quickly as it had started.

"Do you have time to tell me about Aspie's now?"

His eyes lit up. "I don't have to be home 'til ten." Sloane checked her watch; they had a little over an hour.

"Awesome, we're going to my house then."

Chapter 13

"You know someone's going to tell Brick about the Aspie," Noah commented to Liam as they left the den.

"Yeah, I know. I don't know why I was so hard on her. With Joseph and the others missing, it seems to be messing with my lock down." Liam thought about the years of training; learning to control your face, your body language no matter what situation was presented.

"Come on, man. From what I've heard, nothing gets to your lock down. I've heard stories about you taking down half an army of Raks to rescue one guy. I heard about when you were trapped by the ogres and the only way out was by sawing..."

"Yes, yes. I know," Liam interrupted, clearly frustrated as they stepped into the elevator and headed down to the garage level.

They rode in silence for a few moments.

"Wait a minute," Noah looked at Liam, his golden eyes half-lidded, "It was the girl."

"What are you talking about?" Liam turned, eyes narrowed.

"It's the friggin Aspie!" Noah's hearty laugh filled the air. When Liam frowned at him he only laughed more.

"It's *not* the girl," came Liam's stern reply. Noah was wiping the tears off his face and still shaking when they reached his jeep. He gave Liam a slap on the shoulder as he climbed in.

"Good luck with that, man." When the jeep had slipped from sight Liam closed his eyes, took in a cleansing breathe and exhaled slowly. *It was the girl.*

Liam stood dumbfounded for a moment before striding to over to his bike. He stared at it while thoughts roared through his head.

"Hey, there." A soft voice came from behind. Liam flipped around into a defensive position. He'd known too many creatures to trust a harmless sounding voice. Danni stood there, one hand on her hip and the other pushing hair from her face. She smiled and raised her eyes.

"I'm not opposed to being attacked," she said eyeing him intensely. Liam let his defense drop.

"I'm not really in the mood at the moment, Danni."

Before Danni could reply a blue, older model t-bird smoothly pulled into the next parking slot. The windows were so tinted Liam couldn't make out the driver, but he could guess. Liam glanced at Danni only to find that she had vanished.

A moment later the car's engine shut off, leaving a silence only interrupted by the occasional distant traffic. Finally, the door clicked open and a huge man unfolded from the driver's seat. His skin was dark chocolate ebony, yet his eyes were a vibrant green. They stared at

Liam for only a moment before white teeth were displayed in a crooked smile.

"Liam," his resonant voice filled the air like a drum.

"Hey, Brick," Liam said as he held out a hand to his superior. Brick's tree trunk legs brought him over to take the proffered hand. He wasn't nearly as tall as Liam, but his thick, muscled torso and extremities were wide enough to make even Liam think twice about taking him down.

"Did I miss everyone?" Brick asked glancing around the parking lot.

"I'm afraid so," Liam said, "we just wrapped up. Noah went to get some test results and I was heading out to pick up something to eat. We didn't expect you until tomorrow."

Brick smiled again. "I like to come unannounced, but I missed my opportunity this time. There is something I need to talk to you about. Do you mind if we head inside for a few?"

Liam wasn't about to say no so he nodded and lead the way back to the condo. Once inside, Brick looked over the map on the wall. It had been marked with the places and pictures of the missing; Joseph, Caden and Reilly. Then he leaned against the table. It bent slightly under his weight.

"So, tell me about the Aspie."

Liam had anticipated the question, but it didn't stop the cringe he felt inside.

"Based on what she said, she is definitely an Aspie. Based on the problems to hand, I didn't really get into it."

"Hmm," Brick growled, crossing his arms over his chest. Liam watched the table bow just a bit more. "Well, she could be valuable to us and we really should take care of her. No one else will and the Guardianship will want her trained. What we don't have is someone to work with her. The few Aspies they have are on mission. No one's available for another two weeks or so."

"That's fine," Liam said, "as long as I don't have to work with her."

Brick's eyebrow lifted as he stared incredulously at Liam. "I happen to know some of the places you've been sent. Hell, we've taken down some major shit together. You've never batted an eye at an order. Your reputation with women also precedes you." Both eyebrows raised. "Now you're telling me that you can't handle one human girl? What's going on here, Liam?"

Liam sighed, his broad shoulders dropping only slightly as he decided to confide in Brick. "There's something wrong with me, Brick. I've never had this happen before. That girl drives me crazy. She's strong willed and opinionated." Liam paused in thought. "Actually, she's quite impressive. Handling a girl is easy. But this one..." Liam trailed off as he thought of her long legs, pouty lips and fiery nature. Brick cleared his throat.

"What are you talking about?" Brick asked shaking his head. "It's nice to see some passion and not the rock I'm used to dealing with."

"Exactly. There's something wrong with me

and I don't want to waste my skills," Liam continued, "babysitting a new Aspie when I could be helping to find Joseph and the others."

Brick's eye narrowed. Liam shut up.

"She's an Aspie and she's valuable. You have people doing research. You can stare at that map all day long and something may or may not jump out at you. We just don't have enough clues yet to keep everyone busy. There's a shortage of Aspie's and she just might be able to help."

Brick paused and eyed Liam who nodded understanding, if not agreement. Obviously, Brick had been talking to a few people.

"Your orders: First; get her agreement however you need to, then oversee the testing of her abilities. See what she can do. Get someone to take her around and get a feel for her talent. Then *you* test her. We'll go from there. Understood?"

"Yes, Brick," Liam said with as much respect as he could muster.

"And Liam?" Brick gave Liam a hard look, "This one's off limits to you, okay?" Liam nodded.

"Good. Now go."

Liam nodded again and headed back out of the condo. He frowned when he heard the sound of Brick's deep laugh cut off by the door.

THE GUARDIANS

Chapter 14

When they arrived at her house, Sloane quickly threw together some hot chocolate and settled into her favorite purple chair. Keppin sat back on the couch and sipped his loudly. A week ago, Sloane would have laughed in her own face if she thought she would be sitting in her living room, drinking hot chocolate and eagerly anticipating the words of a teenager she had brought home with her. She sighed and gazed into her cup as though the milky swirls would tell a story and unravel her confusions.

"This place is all yours, huh?" Keppin asked, his eyes devouring the room.

"Yep. It's not much but I don't have to share." She waited until Keppin had sucked down half his drink and started to relax a little.

"Okay, Keppin. Lay it on me. What the heck is an Aspie?" Excitement flashed over Keppin's face, his familiar grin spreading as he looked at her.

"It's really awesome," he started. Sloane wondered how much she would get out of him in less than an hour.

"Aspie is short for the Latin word *aspicio* which means 'to see'." Keppin looked at her and she nodded. That was impressive and not something she ever thought she'd hear out of a teenager's mouth.

"A long time ago, and I don't know how long in case you were going to ask me, it was discovered by the group that, uh, you just sort of met," Keppin shrugged, Sloane rolled her eyes and he continued, "anyway, it was discovered that there were some human, uh, people out there that had special abilities. They could see colors around others and it would tell them a lot of stuff. They could see the mood a person was in. Like you!"

Keppin smiled broadly at Sloane. She couldn't help but smile back and nod. *Weird people like me.*

"So anyway, that was the first thing that was noticed, but then they saw that some of the more powerful Aspie's could sense other cool stuff. They could, uh, feel emotion from far away. Like there's this story about this one lady who somehow heard her son struggle and fall in a nearby river. She was able to get help and save him. If she hadn't, the kid would've died!"

"Interesting," Sloane commented as she frowned. She wasn't sure if she'd ever experienced anything like that. A few hazy memories hung about but nothing solid to latch onto. She glanced up at the still grinning Keppin and waved a hand at him to continue.

"Ok, so then it was figured out that some Aspie's could also influence others. Like get them to feel what they want them to feel to get what they want. Pretty cool, huh?"

Sloane cocked her head in thought before speaking, "Let me get this straight. An Aspie, a strong Aspie, can not only read emotion from near and far but can also sway emotion?"

"Yeah! Isn't that cool? Sometimes I wish I was an Aspie." Keppin sighed, a thoughtful grin on his face.

"I only see their emotion but I've never noticed anything far away or ever used it to sway any...wait a minute. I've gotten out of a ton of speeding tickets. Not had even one. And every time I would be thinking *no ticket*. I wonder if that's part of it!" Sloane was starting to get excited.

"Yeah that or maybe it's cuz you're a hot babe." Keppin's eyes got wide the moment the words left his mouth.

"I'll pretend you didn't say that," Sloane said. Keppin nodded, blushing. A glance at the clock told her they were almost out of time.

"Is there anything else? Any other tidbits that might help me?"

"Well, ah, one thing but I don't think you want to hear it."

"Lay it on me. I'm a big girl."

"That's the problem. Aspie's usually have all the powers they're gonna have by the time their ten or so."

Sloane sat back and let that sink in. So maybe she wasn't one of the powerful ones. That was fine, at least she knew what was happening. She hoped that would help her deal with it.

"Ok, then. Well, at least I know what's happening now. Thanks, Keppin."

He nodded at her, not smiling anymore. He was looking around the apartment again, everywhere but at her. Her eyes narrowed.

"Not very good at hiding stuff, are you?"

"What do you mean?" he asked finally looking her way.

"There's something you don't want to tell me."

"Ah, no. That's about everything."

"Spit it out," Sloane commanded.

"Fine. But you asked for it." The smile was gone from his face and his lower lip quivered fleetingly. "If...if we don't find the Aspie's they don't last long."

"And why is that?"

"They usually end up in institutions."

Sloane took in a deep breath and pursed her lips. "I know, Keppin. That one I know."

Chapter 15

While Eric snored quietly, *thank God for that,* Andy thought, he stood at their dresser. The light glow of the lamp illuminated him in the mirror. He wasn't really looking at himself; he was still puzzling over the scene in the alley. Eric had been seriously scared of him. Eric who caught stray spiders and took them outside where they belonged, who had no problem standing up to bullies whether he won or lost. Andy took a hard look at himself. He didn't look like a stranger or a weirdo.

He looked...normal. Andy's bronze colored skin shone gently in the light. He liked to keep his dark, straight hair very short, almost shaved, and although his almond shaped brown eyes could see further and more clearly than anyone else, they looked ordinary. Andy inspected his arms and chest. He was muscular, working out three times a week did that, and he had a feeling if he needed to be strong, really strong, the power would be there. Maybe not normal, but at least normal looking, he thought.

He needed some answers. He had seen other boys ask for help from the counselors and they usually ended up on some drug or another. Andy couldn't understand how people could tell you to say no to drugs and then prescribe a drug with amazingly long lists of side effects and no proof that they improved your mental health. What was worse was if you decided to stop taking the drug you were screwed. Either addicted and having to have them or forced by your counselor anyway for your "own good." Andy wanted to steer clear of that trap and that left him puzzling again. Who could he go to? Then it came to him. He shook his head at the irony.

~~*~~

Andy made sure he was on the list for basketball that morning. He was hoping to run across his 'help' while on the way. Being underage and in an orphanage, took away a lot of the street roaming that a normal kid might be used to. He didn't have the freedom to traipse off on his own to go exploring or do what he needed.

Talking and joking with the other boys as they made their way to the courts he was disappointed when they reached the alley. The last trip was the only time he had seen the bum there. It looked as if Andy had scared him from a return trip. Andy's mood was dark as they hit the courts, but he played none-the-less and was able to forget his troubles momentarily.

After the game Andy, along with several others, hit the water fountain to cool down. As Andy lifted his head up from drinking he spotted motion at a dumpster near the shaded corner of the building next to the park. He moved away from the others and watched curiously as a person poked through some bags in the dumpster. Being faced with a backside Andy couldn't tell if it was who he hoped for, but he watched intensely.

Eric, who had been timid since the alley incident, sidled up next to him and also watched.

"Do you think that might be the weird guy from the alley?" Eric wondered aloud.

"Yeah," Andy answered, "I was curious about what he was going on about."

"I'm curious but not sure I want to know," Eric said quietly. Andy glanced at him, but Eric kept his eyes on the bum.

"I don't know if I want to know but I think I need to," Andy finally said. The bum found something particularly interesting and hunched over it for a time. The rest of the boys were cycling through the water fountain and time was running out.

"Cover for me?" Andy asked, keeping his eyes on Eric. Eric paused, thinking and then finally turned.

"Make it fast though," he said. "If they ask, I don't know where you went." Andy nodded.

"Thanks, man. I owe you one." He turned and jumped the fence separating him and the bum across the way. The bum still had his back to him and had started shuffling through the trash again. When he heard Andy's approach he stopped and straightened slightly. Andy came up next to him, but not too close and peered at him.

The bum peered back.

"Can I help you?" the bum asked through yellowed teeth. It was not who Andy was looking for.

"I guess not," Andy said, disappointed, "I thought you were someone else." The bum stood and stared Andy down for a moment. A flash of recognition crossed his face and he smiled a sly smile that sent a chill down Andy's back. Andy raised a questioning eyebrow.

"You're a phaser," the bum said with a nod like he was affirming something for himself. Andy's raised eyebrow turned into a frown.

"A what?" he asked, bewildered.

"You're a phaser, right? Joe said a phaser scared the pizz out 'em the other day. I'm thinkin' he's talkin' about you."

"Does Joe like to sing to himself?" Andy asked. The bum had already started pushing the trash around again.

"Yep, if that's what you wanna call it."

"Where would I find another one of these phasers?" Andy asked, praying for a direction.

"I seen 'em in the alleys, at night sometimes. Not often but I been around a while. Maybe if yeh hang around an alley you might run into one someday."

Andy rolled his eyes and glanced back at the courts. The boys had already crossed the street and were heading down the alley. Counselor Sam was leading the way, oblivious that he was short one orphan.

"Thanks," Andy said with a sigh. He started

toward the fence when the bum's gravelly voice stopped him short.

"New one in town, he likes him some coffee, he does. Seen 'em with coffee cups downtown few times."

Andy turned to question the bum further, but he had already moved away down the alley and Andy was out of time.

Chapter 16

The sun already had a good start on Sloane. Stepping out of the shower she wrapped a towel around her head, put on her cozy black robe and headed to her bedroom. Halfway there she remembered the leave-in conditioner was sitting on the kitchen counter and about-faced. It was sitting on the counter right next to the gift basket.

She stared at the basket for a long moment. She saw it contained yummy coffee, shortbread and chocolates.

"What. The. Fuck." A glance around the spotless kitchen showed nothing else out of place. *And no note.* The chocolate did it. If she was poisoned by it then it was her time. She grabbed one, discarded its fancy wrapper and bit in. Heading out of the kitchen, she groaned in pleasure.

"Chocolate's not the only thing that'll make you feel like that."

Sloane's hand stopped halfway to her mouth and her head snapped to the living room so fast she pulled a nerve. As her eyes narrowed in pain she recognized her guest. Liam was sitting quite comfortably in her favorite purple velvet chair wearing nothing but a smoker's jacket. Yeah right, in her dreams.

Wearing a green tee, black sweats and flip flops, his skin was flushed like he had just recently...she stopped that thought right there. A small, black bag lay on the floor at his feet. She quickly surveyed the door and observed all the locks in place. The throbbing in her neck eased off.

"Hello, Sloane," Liam said as he stood. "I hope this isn't a bad time." He was tall and still magnificent. Sloane scowled.

"What are you doing in my house?" she demanded angrily. Liam gave a brief smile.

"I stand corrected on the way I handled things the other day. I need to talk to you for a few moments if possible."

"Fine. I would invite you in but oh, look! You already are."

Sloane sat on her white pleather love seat. It was then she noticed the disposable coffee carafe and two of her mugs on the light wood coffee table that separated them. Her eyes narrowed at him. He just smiled and shrugged. "Peace offering?" he asked. Sloane watched as he poured them each a cup.

Liam held one out to her. She looked at it for a moment before asking, "How do you take yours?"

"Any way it comes actually. There are coffee snobs and then there are coffee lovers. I'm definitely the latter."

"All right, well, mine needs cream." Sloane

headed into the kitchen and returned with cream and sugar. When she returned he was back in her chair. She poured cream into her coffee and sat back on the couch. Sipping it she watched Liam add cream and sugar to his. When he was done he leaned back and their eyes met.

"You know what really bothers me?" she asked softly. Liam shook his head.

"What really bothers me is that some of the weirdest, damndest things have happened to me in the last three days and that doesn't bother me. I find a kid in my trunk. I meet an odd group of people who were most definitely scheming, about what I have no idea. I let a teenager explain to me what it is that is wrong, but not really wrong, with me and I believe him, and finally some guy breaks into my house and do I scream? Do I call the cops? No. I sit down and have coffee with him while I'm still in my fucking bathrobe. And the only fucking thing that bothers me is that it doesn't fucking bother me!"

Liam just looked at her. He didn't smile, didn't frown, and just looked at her. After a heavy sigh she sat back and let the caffeine take its toll.

He finally spoke. "Keppin tells me that he told you all about Aspies, at least what he knows?"

Sloane nodded, "Over hot chocolate."

"Over hot chocolate? Well, he failed to mention that detail. I'll make sure he's punished later." Sloane couldn't help but smile.

"So now you know that there's nothing wrong with you, that you possess a completely natural yet rare ability?" Liam waited for her nod and continued, "What he didn't tell you is what we do, correct?"

"Correct. If I may be blunt about it, all this secrecy is kind of weird."

"Touché. Most people don't get to us as fast as you did, Sloane. I don't know anything about you, not what you do for a living, your hobbies, things you support or are against," Liam's face grew serious, "I would like to give you an introduction and let you chew over it for a bit. You could help us. In exchange, we would arrange for you to be trained to handle and use your ability. If you're interested, I will give you a full briefing. If you're not interested you will simply forget that you ever met me, or Keppin."

Sloane wasn't sure if he was joking or not. He wasn't smiling, not even a little.

"You're serious? You can magically make me forget this whole thing ever happened including knowing what I am?"

"I don't really know how to get around deleting all of it." He shrugged. "If it helps, I was ordered to make you the offer."

"That doesn't help." Sloane put her cup on the table, got up and paced the small area behind the love seat. The hallway to her room, the living room and kitchen all felt like they were shrinking down. She stopped in near the front door, hands on her hips, and turned to him.

"My entire life I have wondered what the hell was wrong with me. Why do I see things that others can't? Knowing, *knowing,"* she repeated, "that if I said anything I would be hauled off in a strait jacket before you could say boo. Now I finally know that I have some inherent abilities that are unknown in the broad scheme of things but do exist and you're telling me that I'm going to forget that if I don't do what you want?"

Liam stood and put his hands in his pockets.

"What I'm telling you is that I am part of a group that is unknown to the general population but is protecting them every single day. We would like to share information with you and get your help if you're so inclined. If not, I can't have you running around telling people. The number of people that I keep alive is worth one person's memories. I know they're your memories and you probably don't share that viewpoint, but it's the best I can give you under the circumstances."

"This," Sloane waved her hands toward Liam, "this is what the twilight zone is all about. I'll agree and next thing I know I'll have lost three days of my life and have two heads." Sloane sat back down and rubbed her face. Liam sat back down, the picture of a statue on her favorite chair, watching her silently. Sloane took several breathes before speaking again.

"I want to know," she admitted, "but first, I'd like to get dressed."

"Great. While you're doing that, I have an acquaintance I need to invite over. She'll help protect both our interests."

Sloane glared at him and headed to her room.

Chapter 17

Eric had been called in to Counselor Sam's office that morning just after class had started. Andy sat at the table in the dining hall waiting. Worried, he pushed meatloaf around on his plate while he watched the entry door. He perked up when Eric finally walked sluggishly through the door. Andy watched him make his way slowly through the buffet. Instead of coming to sit with Andy, like his friend had done every day for years, Eric sat at the first available table and began to eat mechanically, paying no heed to anyone around him.

Quickly finishing his meal, Andy got up and with a glance at Eric, headed back to his room. He still had a half hour before lunch was over. Before he made it down the hall, Sam called to him. Andy stopped and turned slowly, heart pounding.

"Andy, would you come see me when lunch is over?" Sam asked with a smile. Andy nodded and then turned back to the hall stairs and went up to the second floor. *First Eric, now me.* He knew what they were doing. He knew Eric must have told them what had happened. He had managed to avoid the drugs for this long; he had no intention of starting now.

Once the door closed behind him, Andy grabbed his backpack and hastily collected up as many of his belongings as possible, stuffing them in just as quickly. His small family picture album fit snugly into the front zippered pocket. His heart was working overtime but started to slow in disbelief when he realized he had no way out. To leave in broad daylight with a backpack at lunchtime would be insane. He'd never make it. Going to the window he shoved his backpack through the bars, letting it rest on the shelf to the left of the window where it would stay hidden. He would figure out how to retrieve it later. Leaning his head on the thick, black bars, he held the bars on either side of his head. Apathy washed over him and he felt the tears start to sting. He imagined himself stepping through the bars to freedom. A vaguely familiar tingle washed over him.

Andy rushed to the dresser mirror and gasped. His skin was churning; different shades of black and gray mixing together in a strange rhythm. He touched his face but it felt the same, solid. Andy leaned onto the dresser to get a closer look and felt his hands slip off the counter. He glanced down to see what had made him slip. His hands were gone! His arms ended just above his wrists and the rest was just gone.

Panicking, Andy pulled away from the dresser but his hands came right along with them, still churning in different dark shades. He put a hand on the dresser and watched it penetrate the surface and sink down into the wood. He did it several more times in awe. Then he had an idea. He raised his hands and looked them over as he turned to the window.

He watched carefully as he reached toward one of the bars and was amazed when his hand passed through the bar as though it wasn't even there. Without a second thought Andy climbed onto the windowsill and started pushing his way through. Andy found himself, miraculously, on the other side of the bars. He went to grab his backpack but his hand went right through it. Puzzled, Andy closed his eyes and wished his hand solid. He opened one eye and looked at his hand. It looked normal. Reaching for the pack again the feel of the rough nylon against his fingers made him sigh in relief.

A stone shelf along the outside of the building made it easy for Andy to get to the corner. On the ground was a group of decorative bushes that Andy and the other orphans had used many times for hide and seek. When Andy reached the corner of the wall he took a deep breath and jumped.

His feet hit the ground next to the wall but behind the bushes, exactly where he had aimed for. He felt a slight jar when he landed, but it was nothing more than if he had jumped from a chair. Excitement surged through him. He felt like a super hero or something.

"Find him!"

Sam's voice sent a chill through Andy. He had almost forgotten that he was in the middle of escaping. He had always liked Sam well enough and had even felt comfortable with him. The betrayal ignited a slow burn of anger.

Without enough understanding of his powers to know what he would look like running through the expansive yard in the front of the building he certainly didn't want to chance being caught, so he waited and watched. It dawned on him that they were searching the building. He heard Sam's voice through his bedroom window.

Realizing that they didn't know where he was, he stood straight up out of the protection of the bushes, turned and walked toward the back of the building, across the short backyard and into the forest behind. He didn't look back. There was nothing to remember.

THE GUARDIANS

Chapter 18

When Sloane came back into the living room wearing comfy gray sweats and a black tee, she found Liam with her new house guest. It was the lady from the meeting. Petite, thin, with platinum blond hair cut just below the chin in uneven layers her blue eyes pierced Sloane's, and then seemed to settle into a dark gray. Before Sloane could comment Liam jumped up from her purple chair.

"Sloane, this is Danni. She's our resident expert on," he paused glancing at Danni, "both preventing and ensuring memory loss."

Sloane raised an eyebrow and looked back and forth between them. "What does that mean exactly?"

Liam shrugged. "In short she's going to cast a spell that ensures our safety and helps preserve your memory before you learn anything else."

"You've got to be kidding," Sloane mumbled as her shoulders dropped in disbelief. She moved to the window at the rear of the living room, rubbing her forehead as she looked out into the small yard. Her squirrel friend dashed from the house to the tree, pausing to meet her eyes, nod and disappear into a hidden hole.

Dropping her hand to her side Sloane tried to interpret the nod. Her disbelief turned to belief when she realized, like a bullet in the head, that she was not the only one on the planet who was gifted.

She turned around to find that neither Liam nor Danni had moved. They stood quietly, waiting. Liam's height dwarfed the small lady next to him. Sloane thought she saw a glimmer of motion in the lady, some type of aura that wanted to show itself but was forced back into hiding. Something beyond the odd light green that blended closely to her.

Observing Danni, Sloane realized that she was indeed a lady. Despite her demeanor and youthful clothes, ripped jeans and half shirt, she was a lot older than she was letting on. Somehow that made Sloane feel a little more comfortable.

Sloane looked at Liam. He made her emotions twist and change like the desert sand. She wanted to trust his judgment, to trust him. He stood completely still before her, no more motion then a statue, except his eyes. They caressed her face from across the room. The usual calm she felt around Gray One's settled around her like a hazy sunset and she glanced at Danni in time to see her watching Liam with an adoring gaze. The gaze turned to a frown when she realized Sloane was watching and any hint of emotion was vanquished.

The calm broke, letting the sounds of the house, the birds outside and the rap blaring from a car in the distance roar into her mind. She had chosen her plan of action.

"I will do this, but I have one request," she announced. Liam moved, this time slowly, and stood before her looking down.

"Yes?" he asked softly. Sloane's skin started to burn, her mouth turning to sandpaper as she felt the intensity of his gaze penetrate her very core. She leaned around him to glance at Danni. Danni hadn't moved. Her body was tense, hands on her hips as she stared daggers at Sloane. Then she smiled, sending chills down Sloane's spine.

Looking back at Liam, straight into his eyes, she whispered, "You trust her?"

Without breaking the gaze, he whispered back, "She's been working with the crew here for several years and they speak highly of her skills."

Sloane nodded. This time she spoke clearly, to be sure she was overheard. "Whatever she does, she has to do it so you can see and hear everything." Danni laughed.

"That won't be a problem," Danni spoke for the first time. Sloane noticed the hint of a foreign accent, maybe Scottish or Irish. Her voice was high pitched and soft at the same time. Sloane vaguely remembered hearing Danni speak to Keppin when she was blindfolded.

"Okay, then let's get this out of the way," Sloane said trying to mask her fear.

"It'll be fine," Liam said and smiled. He put a hand on her shoulder, sending warmth down her spine and guided her to the loveseat.

Sloane watched as Danni dumped the contents of a pouch on to the table and prepared for the spell.

A beautiful metal object that looked like a cast iron incense stand, was set right. It had a round top where a bowl would sit and an empty area below where Danni placed a white candle. The legs twisted down to sit on the table and then curled out in spirals with a colored gem set at each end, facing upward. Danni set a worn pottery bowl into its top. She picked up a small burlap bag, loosened the drawstring and poured the contents into the bowl.

"Why not use a plastic bag?" Sloane wondered aloud, "seems like it would be easier."

"A plastic bag would leach chemicals into the mixture; it can seriously alter a spell." Danni's condescending tone sparked anger in Sloane's stomach but she stayed silent. Liam sat down to her right which made her feel a bit better.

"It looks like crushed herbs," Liam commented, taking the thought from Sloane's mind. She allowed a small smile. He was trying to put her at ease and it was working.

"Lavender, sea salt, fennel, hyssop, eucalyptus and a touch of mandrake to be exact," Danni said to Liam. "Each herb contains an element of protection and preservation that aids the spell."

Liam made a small grunt of acknowledgment. "Besides," Danni continued, "it smells divine." She smiled at him. Sloane wanted to burn holes into her with heat-seeking eyes.

Danni placed the bowl on the table in front of Sloane and slid a small dagger across the table.

"Both of you need to prick your fingers and put at least five drops of blood into the bowl."

Sloane's head flew up. "What?"

Danni lifted a shoulder. "It won't work otherwise. It needs blood from the guarded and blood from the *outsider*." Danni pursed her lips distastefully. Instead of rolling her eyes or making a comment that would increase the tension between them, Sloane turned to Liam. He picked up the dagger and inspected it. After a moment he leaned forward and reached behind and beneath his shirt.

Sloane was surprised to see him pull out a sleek, rounded black knife. He stabbed his thumb and held it over the bowl. Sloane watched, mesmerized, as the thick red drops soaked into the herbs. When he was done he stuck his thumb in his mouth. Sloane couldn't help but smile at that and he smiled back around his thumb.

Sloane quickly went to the kitchen, grabbed a clean cloth and wet part of it. She took the cloth back with her and held out her hand for the knife. Liam gave it to her, handle first and she wiped the blade clean and dried it.

Sitting with the knife in one hand, Sloane looked at Liam. He nodded so she brought the blade to her thumb, closed her eyes and gently shoved. The knife was so sharp she barely felt it. Blood welled up immediately and she held it out over the bowl. Liam took the knife back and wiped it down as she counted out her drops and watched them seep into the herbs with his. She smiled at the idea that they were mingling energy somehow. Liam handed her the towel. She took it and put pressure on the cut even though she knew it would heal up quickly without help. Danni took a flat stick and stirred the bowl.

"What's your full name?" she asked.

"Sloane Jacobs."

"Ok, I'm going to light the candle and you'll need to breathe in the fragrance. Don't be alarmed at anything, you won't be hurt," Danni said to Sloane.

"Ok," Sloane said softly. Danni lit the candle and watched it for a moment before nodding to Sloane. A vaporous mist wafted up from the bowl. Sloane leaned in and took a deep breath. The smell was lovely! It reminded her of happy days; sunsets, father reading her a book, baking cookies with mom. Closing her eyes, a warm peace settled over her, an indistinct veil covering her surroundings. Sloane's breath became slow and even as she relaxed, but her awareness of Liam and Danni remained strong. She opened her hand and felt Liam's fold around it. It was comforting and she giggled when she realized it was she who had commanded it.

Danni's voice came through clearly. "Sloane Jacobs, you will hear of worlds and creatures you have never imagined to be real or true. You will not speak of them to anyone unless they already know. Do you understand?"

Sloane nodded and felt Liam's hand tighten on hers.

"Sloane Jacobs, if you speak of these worlds

or creatures to anyone not previously knowing, your memory of these worlds, people and creatures will vanish. Do you understand?"

Sloane nodded again.

"Sloane Jacobs, you will never harm the members of Liam's group, The Guardianship, or their allies. You will protect them as you can and use your power to its fullest capacity. Do you understand?"

Sloane nodded once more. She glowed with trust and security. *Finally. People who understood.*

~~*~~

Liam gripped Sloane's hand and watched her in the trance or whatever it was. She was aware and yet influenced by Danni's words. He observed Danni carefully. He'd been through these types of spell castings before but he *didn't* trust Danni, didn't know her story. There was something niggling at his mind, but he hadn't placed a finger on it yet.

After Sloane had given the last nod, Liam knew it was almost over. Danni reached out and drew a symbol on Sloane's forehead but no words were used. He would have to find out what the symbol meant later.

Sloane let out a deep sigh. Liam felt his heart tighten and he had to smile, she looked so at peace. And she was so devastatingly lovely.

Then she changed.

She took in a frightened breath, her eyes flew

open and he knew intuitively she saw something he couldn't. He moved to hold her hand with both of his as he watched the color drain from her face.

Her mouth started moving but no sound could be heard. Her lips started to turn a light blue color. Giving her hand a squeeze he felt nothing in response. Her hand just lay in his, cold and lifeless.

Liam turned to Danni. She sat on the edge of the table staring in shock at Sloane, her mouth slightly ajar, her eyes churning between blue and gray. Feeling his attention, she turned and shook her head. "I don't know," she mouthed.

Chapter 19

Liam blew out the candle while Danni opened the windows and doors to let the fresh air cleanse the apartment.

Liam was freaking out inside. He had never seen a spell go wayward like this. He could see that Danni was spooked herself. Guessing her to be over two hundred years old, he would have thought she had seen everything by now. She packed up her supplies while he sat and held Sloane's hand, watching her face for any change.

He took his left hand and ran it down her back, feeling a powerful protectiveness fill him. He pushed his feelings through his arm; protect, calm, affinity before resting his hand on the back of her smooth neck. Her damp hair lay still on the back of his hand.

Almost immediately the cold lifeless hand he held in his started to warm and the blue drained from her lips, leaving them a flushed pink. Her eyelids fluttered and she let out a long sigh.

Liam quickly pulled his hand away from her neck. Sloane pulled her hand from his and rubbed her face. When she stopped she turned to Liam and smiled.

Liam grinned back, holding his relief close.

"Are we all done now?" Sloane asked, her eyes bright. "That was neat."

Liam looked at Danni, who stood by the front door, her bag in hand.

"All done," she said as she opened the door, "see you later."

Liam stood up but she had closed the door behind her. He knew if she didn't want to be found she wouldn't be. He would have to talk to her later. Whatever had happened, it scared her.

"She's very odd," Sloane commented. Liam chuckled and Sloane stood with an extra spring in her movement. *Joy?* Liam wondered.

"I'm going to get some coffee and then I can't wait to hear more," Sloane said. Liam watched her smile fade when she saw his face. He quickly pulled it up a few notches.

"Is there enough for two cups?" he asked curling a lip. He watched her mouth turn up again, the light in her eyes seemingly brighter.

"Sure," she said and headed to the kitchen.

Liam's eyes fell on the bloody towel. He glanced to the kitchen door as he rolled the towel up and slid it into his backpack. If for any reason he couldn't get answers out of Danni, he would find them himself.

Chapter 20

The warehouse was damp and muggy and smelled like old sneakers and rancid oil. Andy sank down in a corner exhausted, hungry and lonely. Everything he owned was in the backpack sitting next to him.

He rubbed the sweat off his face only to have it instantly replaced. *Think, think!* He had to figure out a plan and he had to be discrete; the police and who knew who else would be looking for him. Andy held his hands up and thought about the shadows in his skin. He watched as they changed, becoming transparent swirls of darkness. Despite his situation, he allowed a small smile. It shouldn't be too hard to stay concealed.

He would need water and food soon. He knew no one, had no cash and was hiding in an empty warehouse. Andy leaned his head against the wall behind him and closed his eyes. Images of his parents, laughing and smiling, came easily.

He watched as his father gave his mother a look that could melt butter and then turn to Andy. His father's smooth, dark face went grim.

"You're a survivor my son. The very blood in your veins promises that. What it will do for you is

yet to be seen but make the most of it. Make me proud."

Andy started awake. The warehouse was a sauna now, the sun having finished its afternoon rise. Andy's shirt stuck to him like papier-mache and the stagnant air brought no relief from the heat.

Andy knew two things. He needed to handle food and water and he needed help. His only lead, downtown Clearwater coffee shops, was vague. Andy wasn't happy about it, but he knew what he needed to do.

~~*~~

"He escaped, sir."

"Who escaped, Sam? Make it fast, I have things to do."

"The boy I told you about. The one who heals himself."

"Ah. When and where did he escape? Did you do something foolish?"

"I brought in his friend, Eric. He told me that he saw something happen to Andy. Something that scared him. He described it as a flicker, that Andy's body flickered."

"Now that's interesting. What did you do with Eric?"

"I prescribed him Paxil. He calmed down almost immediately."

"Good. Also give him Zoloft and Zyprexa at night. He'll take care of himself soon enough," the doctor laughed, "or he'll take care of someone else and then he'll be locked away safe."

"Isn't that a bit extreme, sir?"

"Extreme, Sam? If you don't do as I ask, I will show you extreme myself."

"Yes, sir."

"You've contacted the authorities?"

"Yes."

"Good. When did you see him last?"

"This morning."

"Ok. Send over a picture of this boy you've lost. I want him."

Chapter 21

"Ok, so you brought up an interesting point earlier." Sloane sat on the couch with her hair hanging loosely and a second cup of coffee in her hand. "You don't know anything about me, nothing. So what makes you think I can help?"

Liam sat in her purple chair, amusement on his face. She raised an eyebrow at him and waited.

"Aspies are generally severe introverts or crazy," he paused and cocked his head thoughtfully. "They're not really crazy of course, but no one believes them so they kind of just go that route, which is very unfortunate. Your hobbies are probably books, computer games, chat rooms, puzzles, or any manner of quiet, singular activities. Your job is probably something where you don't deal much with people. As far as the things you support or are against," he shrugged, "that's a matter of how much schooling you managed to retain while fighting against your natural talent and your own morals."

"Geez, I'm like an open book to you people," she whispered.

"What do you do for a living, Sloane?" he

asked, genuinely curious.

Sloane had to smile. "I drive a school bus."

"Really? That's one I haven't heard before. I had wondered."

It was Sloane's turn to shrug. "Most kids haven't had their hearts torn out yet and life hasn't knocked them around so badly. It's easier to be around their emotions. They're so creative and upbeat. Plus, I take summers off." She laughed.

Liam looked thoughtful for a moment before continuing, "We don't find many Aspies who are in as good a condition as you are, Sloane. It's rare. The reason you can help us is in the very nature of your talent. We can help you to understand it, become comfortable with it and you can help us by using it. It's quite simple really. I'm on a project right now where you could be a beneficial part of the team. You could save many lives."

Sloane closed her eyes so she wouldn't have to look at him or everywhere but at him, while she thought this out. Getting help from this group, from him, could be a dream come true. Her entire life had been a dogged search for answers while avoiding people as much as humanly possible. Growing up, she had never quite fit in. Sure, she was able to fudge it, but then it wasn't true, it wasn't real. In a group like this, she could potentially just be herself. But, there had to be a catch.

"You seem like a fairly capable bunch. What could I possibly do for you that you can't handle yourself?"

"We would handle it eventually, but your skills would help us sort out the situation in a much more expedient fashion."

"Is it ethical? I mean, you're not planning on having me identify types of people so you can off them or anything, right?"

He laughed, a deep joyful howl. Sloane pulled her head back in surprise as he shook. She had never seen him really laugh. Her jaw dropped slightly before she grinned in amusement.

"We're the good guys, I'll tell you that much," he finally said as he stood up. "I have to be somewhere now but we can talk more later if you want to take up the offer." He handed her a white index card with a number written neatly on it. "Give me a call when you're ready." Then he walked past her. She heard the locks click and the door snick closed behind him.

Relief washed over her and she slumped back into the seat. Rubbing her face, maybes and could-be's slugged through her mind. She already knew she wanted to do this, but he had given her so little information to work with. No job description, no group description either, for that matter. He just kept dangling that carrot in front of her. Well, fine, she thought. She didn't really know how much longer she would last on her own and at least this way she could have a group who understood what she was. If it killed her, at least she would go out knowing she wasn't deserving of a lobotomy.

Sloane tossed the index card on the table and

went to find something besides chocolate to eat. A glance in her fridge reminded her that she'd waited long enough and needed a trip to the store, eating more than toast and almond butter might be nice this week. She grabbed a pack of saltines and settled into her favorite chair, delighting in the warmth and musky essence left from Liam's presence. Tucking her legs, she perched her laptop on her knees and checked her small Amazon store. She had always loved collecting dragon statues and figurines and had started selling them periodically for extra cash, her pay as a bus driver being meager. The index card stared at her from the table where she'd left it.

"Aspicio," she said aloud. "Hi, I'm Sloane and I'm an Aspie. No, I'm not psychotic, I actually am a something. Not just any something. I'm an Aspie."

"Aspie," she whispered once more and smiled.

On the one hand, she wanted to call Liam immediately, but he'd been gone all of ten minutes. On the other hand, she thought, she needed to get some work done. More importantly, she felt the need to make him wait. His annoying confidence and distance from her situation ground her nerves. One moment he seemed like he cared a little bit and the next he was cold and distant. Now on the third hand, Sloane giggled to herself as she realized that she had three hands now, she didn't know what he was up against or what he did. Maybe his group was in charge of ensuring that there weren't mass genocides. Or maybe it was a special team that took down terrorists or something really cool and scary like that.

Her hand was itching to pick up the phone. Maybes never did anyone any good. A glance at her screen brought a happy noise from her lips. Someone had gone dragon crazy and bought half of her store! With a last glance at the card she decided to get some work done and call him in the morning.

~~*~~

For the first time since her mother went weird, Sloane felt peaceful. She lay on her bed with the drapes open, the moon shining down and a squirrel gazing in.

Sloane sat up thankful she had on a tee and underwear. The squirrel met her gaze. A movement caught her eye and she broke the face-off only to see a green lizard, inches from the squirrel, staring intently at her.

The lizard looked over at the squirrel and its mouth moved. Sloane frowned. The squirrel glanced over at the lizard, shook its head and again met Sloane's stare. It smiled at her, she thought, and waved.

Sloane decided that despite what Liam said she may not be as sane as he seemed to think. She leaned forward and flipped the lock on the window. She pulled it open from left to right certain that would get them to go away.

But they didn't. Instead they both stepped gingerly over the sill and sat on the inside of the window. Sloane was not worried about the lizard so much but squirrels were not known for being nice and cuddly. They were nutty and sometimes they carried diseases.

"What do you want?" she directed to the squirrel.

He wasn't the one who answered.

"Actually, we..." The lizard never got to finish. The squirrel biffed him out the window with a strong back leg. Sloane backed away a bit, surprised at the amazing detail of her psychotic break.

The squirrel smiled, it's big front teeth making Sloane back up a little bit more. Quickly closing its mouth, it nodded and scampered out the window and into the darkness.

Sloane closed the window, making sure to lock it, and lay back down, not nearly as content. She drifted off to sleep, but images of squirrels, lizards and a little boy being slapped around by his father haunted her.

~~*~~

Liam sat on the corner of her back fence, his shifting skin blending him into invisibility in the darkness. He had arrived just as she'd climbed into bed and watched the odd events transpire before him. To say this Aspie was different was an understatement.

The desire to break in and watch her sleep

started to creep in, signaling that it was time to leave. He shook himself, vaulted off the fence and took to the sky. He would catch some Z's just as soon as he sent a request to HQ for more information on Aspies.

Chapter 22

The darkness was Andy's cover as he slipped easily through the wall and into the convenience store. The air inside was cool on his skin and he shivered happily to get out of the heat. He felt bad breaking in, but he really didn't know what else to do. Giving up and dying wasn't an option.

Shoving as many water bottles into his bag as he could fit, he got a plastic bag and filled it with jerky, a couple of sandwiches and a bag of chips. He couldn't help grabbing a hacky sack as he made his way back through the wall.

Blending with the shadows as much as he could, several blocks away he removed the old hat and coat he had borrowed from a transient he'd met near the warehouse. He planned to return them and find somewhere else to stay. The heat was getting to be too much and it hadn't even been a day yet.

Chapter 23

Sloane started to wonder again if this life was worth it. Forcing herself to shower before she made the call, she finally felt the nightmares fade away. A cheese stick and a couple of B vitamins helped to strengthen her resolve.

She picked up her phone and reached for the white card.

The noise crashed into her head without warning. Abruptly her apartment shrunk, and the air was hard to breath. Tears. Pain. Fear. *Unwelcome*.

She felt soft hands on her face, murmurings she couldn't quite make out. More fear. Then anger.

Then it was just gone.

Sloane found herself crumpled on the floor next to the coffee table, tears still streaming down her face. Through blurred vision she saw the card and picked up the phone that had fallen to the ground.

Chapter 24

Andy stood in the alley near the entrance to Café Bliss. He had already hit Starbucks and Indigo but neither of them had alleys nearby. He had perked up and become a bit more hopeful when he found that Café Bliss did. It was almost ten, closing time for the shop, but he stood his ground.

He was kicking a hacky sack around when his next victim showed up. A hugely muscled, bald biker-looking guy turned into the alley with a coffee in hand.

"Excuse me," Andy said as the dude started to walk by. The guy stopped and looked him up and down, making Andy step back.

"What?" the guy answered slightly amused.

"Do you know where I can find a phaser?"

"Sure man. There's a novelty shop two streets over. They sell a ton of Star Trek memorabilia. Are you a fan?"

Andy smiled. "Nah, man. That wasn't totally what I had in mind. Though I do like Star Trek."

"Sorry then," the guy answered. He gave Andy a look like he had escaped the local prison then continued down the alley. Andy watched until the biker had exited the other end just in case the guy felt like bringing down an escapee. Andy's heart started to sink. He must have talked to at least thirty people that day and gotten nowhere.

Two guys came around the corner talking quietly and holding coffees. One more shot and he would head back to the dreaded warehouse. As soon as they reached him and started to pass he mumbled. "You know about phasers?"

One of the guys stopped abruptly and looked at him, blue eyes narrowed to slits. Andy's heart jumped. The guy had bright red hair. He was exceptionally tall and lean, but built, and there was no question he could kick Andy's ass. Either Andy was going down or the guy knew something. Andy glanced at the other guy who just looked confused. Andy suddenly understood.

"Never mind, man. I was trying to work out some electronic stuff for school and needed help."

The confused guy stopped looking confused and half a smile appeared. He waved a thumb toward the red headed guy. "Electronics is this guy's forte," he commented.

The redhead grunted some kind of confirming answer. He cocked his head at Andy and really looked him over. The guy had some crazy red hair, Andy thought but held his head high during the inspection, just like he did at the orphanage when the government people or doctors came by. The guy looked him over for so long he thought that maybe it was time to get lost, but when the guy seemed to relax a bit, a small hope surged Andy into action. He pulled the hacky sack from his pocket and threw it toward the tall man. In Andy speed. He held his breath. If his gut was wrong, he was about to get his ass kicked.

The guy's arm moved and when it stopped, the hacky sack was gripped in his hand. Andy noticed that the guy had barely moved, only what was necessary. He had also used his body as a shield so that the other guy couldn't see his motion. Not just anyone would have been able to do that. The relief Andy felt was overwhelming. He let his shoulders droop and finally exhaled.

"Please," he pleaded. He didn't know where else to go. This was his only hope. He prayed to whatever God might be listening as their eyes locked. The guy tossed the ball back, in a normal speed, and barely nodded.

"Meet me here Sunday night at eight. I'll see if I can help you." He smiled at Andy and turned, nodding at the other guy. They continued down the alley without looking back.

Andy bolted out of the alley and practically skipped toward the warehouse.

~~*~~

Liam turned to his companion and pointed a thumb to the end of the alley where the boy has disappeared, "He must be hard up for a mentor."

Dr. Zach Maynord laughed. An average looking guy, average height, brown eyes, brown hair, neither over weight nor thin his appearance was misleading as far as Liam was concerned. The man was a genius. Noah had introduced them and they had just been discussing the findings from the toxicology test on the syringe. Though the doc didn't know it, Liam was alarmed. The boy's interruption did little to appease him.

"Thank you very much for the coffee," Dr. Maynord said as he shook Liam's hand, "I hope I was able to help. Must be some very interesting research you're doing."

"It is," Liam said knowing the doc was not stupid, "very. Thanks again for your help."

They parted company and Liam headed back to the den to fill in Brick and the others. They were not going to be happy.

Chapter 25

Liam was waiting for everyone to settle into chairs when his phone rang. Ryan and Kam were preparing coffee in the kitchen while the others got comfortable.

He could barely make out Sloane's whisper.

"Help me."

"What's wrong?" he asked, concern threading through his nerves.

Her voice was rough and her words were mingled with sniffles. The desire to rush to her aid was an annoyance that he brushed away. He was preparing to deliver the results of his discussion with Dr. Zach. Noah stood beside him at the table waiting.

"I'm sorry I called you like this. I'm fine, really, but I do want to meet up and learn more," she told him.

Liam knew she was lying. He never understood why women didn't just cough it up. They always had to play some mind game.

"All right, I'll send someone over with a meeting place for tomorrow."

"Ok, bye," she whispered and hung up. Liam looked at his phone perplexed for a fraction of a second before stuffing it into his pocket.

~~*~~

"The syringe contained two drugs, lithium and Sarin. Lithium is generally prescribed by doctors and psychiatrists. The list of side effects is shocking, even to me, but the ones that caught my attention were tiredness, loss of coordination, muscle weakness and blackouts."

Liam paused and looked over his audience. Brick, who was sitting backward on a dining room chair, nodded, his face grim. Danni, who had been missing since the mishap with Sloane, had shown up just as they were starting the meeting. She said nothing and just sat on the couch with her legs pulled up, hugging them while carefully avoiding Liam's eyes.

Kam and Ryan sat on either side of Danni. Kam's eyes watched Liam intently while Ryan kept glancing at Danni appreciatively. Liam stood off to the side leaning against the wall, while Keanan, Keppin's brother and a currently inactive Guardian, sat crossed legged on the floor in front of the couch.

"Sarin is a poison," Liam continued. "It was designed for use in wars and comes in many forms including liquid. In low doses it will make you uncomfortable; runny nose, coughing, headache, that type of thing. In high doses it can cause blackouts, paralysis and lung failure.

"One of the interesting things about Sarin is that it dissipates into the air quickly. We were lucky to have found it in the syringe at all. There were just trace amounts left so we don't actually know how much was there to start. There was one other ingredient in this concoction that is worse than both of those put together."

Brick frowned and the couch creaked as Kam leaned forward. "What could be worse?" Keanan mumbled. Liam's let his eyes rest upon him for a moment before meeting Brick's grim face.

"Our blood."

Chapter 26

A vaguely familiar Gray One showed up at her door an hour after her break down. They were height for height and she looked in to eyes so brown they were almost black. His weathered face was scarred with a deep crescent running from his left temple down to his chin. She was wondering what could have done that when he smiled. He had perfect white teeth.

Sloane smiled back. She couldn't help it really. He looked her up and down and handed her an envelope.

"Thank you," she said. He nodded and left without a word.

Sloane closed the door and opened the note. It had a place and time written in perfect block letters.

She wondered briefly if Liam could write that neatly as she hunkered down to watch movies for the rest of the day. Anything to keep her mind off everything.

Halfway through *The Chronicles of Riddick* the room closed in on her. She cringed into her chair in anticipation of the pain. Everything went dark then her cheek exploded with the pain of a heavy blow. She cradled her face and pulled her knees to her chest letting the tears flow. Regret and sorrow flowed through her like champagne on New Year's Eve. The throbbing in her cheek started to ease as an unseen hand pressed something cool against it.

When Sloane woke up the TV was silent. Two hours had passed. She sat up and felt her face. There was no bruising, nothing. It was like it had never happened.

~~*~~

The next day Sloane woke feeling better than she had in days. A restful, nightmare-free evening and an exciting day ahead certainly helped. She cleaned up her apartment and even decided to clean out her car. When she opened the door, a foul smell greeted her. Wrinkling her face, Sloane pulled the smoothie that her mother had given her from the cup holder. She tossed it, cup and all, in to the trash bin. She had forgotten all about it with Keppin's call yesterday. She smiled to herself. She had been appeasing her mother for years drinking those things week after week. It was freeing somehow to have missed one. Sloane let the car air out while she got ready for her meeting with Liam.

Arriving ten minutes early at the restaurant, Sloane found that Liam had beaten her there. He was sitting at the last booth in the back facing the door. Sloane waved and headed over. She was almost at the table when he stood and gestured for her to sit. Her face flushed and she kept her head down as she slid into the booth.

"Would you like something to eat?" Liam asked. He looked good. Blue jeans, army green tee, black biker boots.

"No, thank you, I already ate."

"Now why'd you go and do that?"

"Not much into fast food," she said and lifted her shoulders. Liam looked at her for a moment and then got in line. When he returned he put chips, a bag of apples and a soda in front of her. She looked up at him eyebrow raised. He shrugged.

"Can't have you sitting there just watching me eat now can I?"

Sloane gave a partial smile and shrug. To her surprise, he slid into the booth right next to her leaving the seat across from them very empty. She took a sip of her drink while he unwrapped a foot-long sub and dug in. He'd gotten her root beer, her soda of choice. Interesting.

"I imagine when you're done eating there will be some explanation as to why I'm here?"

Liam nodded at her as he chewed. Luckily he wasn't one of those talk-with-your-mouth-full types. While she waited, Sloane opened the apples and started to chew a tasteless slice. She avoided even a glance at any of the people coming in to order. She was glad that most of them got takeout. When Liam finished he stood up and tossed his wrapper into the trash. Before sitting back down he pulled a small notebook and a pen from his back pocket and handed them to her.

This time she raised both eyebrows and waved the notepad at him. If he was any more informative, things would start to erase from her mind.

"We're going to people watch," he said. Sloane's mouth fell open. She caught it and let out a disgruntled noise.

"That is something I hate more than anything in the world, save maybe politics and child molesters. Why on earth did you bring me here for that? Can't you handle that on your own?"

Liam touched her hand sending shooting stars through her veins. She still felt it even after he moved away. *Focus.*

"I need you," he started causing a thrill to zip down her spine, "so I can find out what you see and what it means to you. Plus, the sooner you start confronting people the easier it will get to be around them."

"Easy for you to say," she grumbled. She sat back, propping her feet on the bench across from them and folded her arms across her chest.

"Don't think I didn't notice your constant avoidance of people," Liam said softly. He took the notepad, opened it up and then he too leaned back. Sloane didn't want to, but she noticed he was not touching her, which was hard to do since they were two tall, broad shouldered adults squished into a small booth. She wondered if her deodorant was working.

"Okay, guy behind the counter. What's his color?" he asked. Sloane looked over.

"He's yellow with a hint of red."

"And what's yellow with a hint of red mean to you?"

"He's bored."

"Alright, chick behind the counter."

"Did you just say 'chick'?"

"Pardon me, female behind the counter."

"She's dark yellow."

"And what's dark yellow?"

"Umm. Like depressed or sorry...sad."

"Ok, customer up front in the gray shirt."

Liam took notes on all of it. He really did have neat handwriting.

That was how the next two hours went. Sloane's back was getting sore and she had to roll her neck periodically to keep it from hurting. Liam finally put down the notepad, his comments hidden from view.

"You can really see them clear as day," he commented. "Well, I think that's good enough for today."

Sloane breathed in deep and blinked a few times to bring her back to the living. She finally turned and smiled at Liam.

"That wasn't so bad. Having someone who doesn't think I'm a lunatic certainly makes it easier."

Liam smiled back. "There's a few of us wandering around. For the most part all of us 'Gray Ones'," he made quotes with his long fingers, "will know what you're about."

"Cool. That's good to know." Sloane made the motions to clean up the table and leave. She wasn't certain, but she thought he was looking at her. She certainly wasn't going to check. She would maybe keep her eyes out for *other* Gray Ones. This one was in a class of his own.

"Tomorrow I'm going to have you work with Noah. You'll hit two or three places starting at eleven. Will that work for you?"

"Sure."

"Good. You'll spend about forty-five minutes in each place. Noah will pick you up. I'm hoping you'll get comfortable enough, it seems to me you know your stuff, so that I can take you out on an undercover outing.

"Sounds interesting."

"We'll see," he commented as he stood up. He tucked the notepad into one pocket while he pulled keys out of the other. Sloane followed and they headed to the door. Liam held the door for her and then waved as he headed one way to his motorcycle and she went the other.

Sloane sat in her car, soaking up the heat and thawing from the chill of the restaurant. She had wanted to tell him about the visions. She needed to talk to someone desperately, but fear of getting any closer to him had kept her mouth shut. Not only did her hormones perk up whenever he was around, she was actually starting to like him and that was bad. Very bad. At least she was pretty sure it was. Maybe.

Chapter 27

The next day she tried on three different outfits before deciding it was a stupid thing to worry about and put on her standard jeans and tee. She was just trying to find her black sweater, so she wouldn't freeze to death in the restaurants, when she heard the bell.

"Come in," she yelled from her room. Finding it on the floor of the closet, she shook it out and tied it around her waist. When she walked into the living room, Noah was standing just inside the front door. She recognized him from the secret meeting. His hue was different than the others. It was gray but there was an added soft white glow close to his skin. *Curious* she thought. She met his gaze and caught herself from stumbling as she made her way over to him. His strange dragon eyes never left her and showed nigh a hint of her falter.

He held out a hand. Sloane took it and smiled.

"All set?" he asked, his low voice warm and cozy like a blanket. Sloane liked him instantly.

She nodded and scooped up her purse as they headed out the door.

They rode in silence at first. Noah was a smooth driver and despite the stick shift, she barely felt the Jeep move from one gear to another. She wondered how much torque it had. She was also curious about Noah. She noticed he didn't have a wedding ring and wondered if he had someone or if he was a man whore like Liam. *No. Out, out, out,* she told herself. She was not going to think about *him.*

"So how did you get stuck with me today?"

He shrugged. "I offered."

"Huh. Well, I only just found out about this stuff myself."

He smiled, though his eyes stayed on the road. "That's part of what makes it interesting."

Sloane couldn't help but smile. "Okay, I have to ask," she said, "do you surf?"

"Occasionally. Why?"

"You kind of have that look about you. Except for your eyes. I'm sure you hear all the time how unusual they are."

He chuckled, "You have no idea."

Sloane sighed as she settled into the seat and enjoyed the cool AC. "It is so nice to sit here like a normal person and chat and not be able to read you like a book. So refreshing."

"I can't even imagine having to deal with that on a constant basis. Apparently, you're holding up better than most with all of this."

"So I've been told," Sloane murmured and looked out the window. "Many times I've wondered how I've lived this long and still kept some semblance of sanity. Many times."

"Well, wonder no longer. You were meant to meet us."

Sloane looked at him thoughtfully. "Maybe so."

~~*~~

It was a restaurant she didn't frequent, but certainly nicer than a fast food joint.

They walked in, neither saying anything and sat in a far corner booth with a good view of the entry. Another notepad appeared from a pocket and as they sat, she observed, telling him everyone's hue.

As she studied one suited man who sat alone at a booth, vague and random images flashed in her mind. She frowned while the images flipped through her mind like a slide show. She watched the man take hasty drinks of the golden liquid from his short glass. Noah noticed.

"What's happening?" he asked softly. Sloane waited until the images stopped flowing before answering.

"This might sound weird, but I can somehow see what he's thinking about."

"Really?" he was intrigued. "Like what?"

"Well," Sloane glanced at Noah. He was beautiful in his own right. And sweet. But besides the affinity she had felt instantly, her hormones lay dormant. "He keeps thinking of two women. And judging by the ring on his finger, one of them shouldn't be a part of the equation."

"Ah. So, he's been unfaithful and it's eating him alive." Noah's soft voice was oddly comforting.

"Exactly," Sloane acknowledged. "I can see his hue, a yellow so light it's almost white tinged with red. He's nervous, anxious. I've never been able to actually *see* images before, like reading his mind."

"Maybe using your skill more frequently is making them more accessible."

"I guess that could be," Sloane propped an elbow on the table and rested her head thoughtfully on the palm of her hand, "I've avoided it my whole life and here I've used it more in the last two days than ever. That or Danni's spell."

"Interesting," Noah said as he watched the man slowly get drunk. Sloane searched his pained face and made a decision.

"Noah?" she asked and he turned to look at her. She gazed into his otherworldly eyes. They so reminded her of dragons. It made her smile. Noah raised both eyebrows. Sloane shook her head.

"Your eyes can be distracting," she commented with nothing behind it except the truth. He nodded.

"So I've heard," he said, a smile playing at his lips.

"I've been seeing things," she blurted out. "Weird things that don't make sense, and yet do. I know Liam said," her heart fluttered when she said his name, "that I wasn't crazy, but I think I might be a little bit."

"Whoa. Slow down there," Noah touched her arm. The concern on his face warmed her and gave her that cozy in a blanket feeling. She closed her eyes and breathed out slowly as realization hit like a tidal wave and rode down to her toes, ebbing and flowing with knowledge. Noah cared. He was genuinely interested and concerned. She was so unaccustomed to the idea that she sat shocked for a moment, hiding her face from him.

Her thoughts turned to Liam. What was it about him? She couldn't tell if he was coming or going. One minute he was interested and the next, he was the blank faced boss-man. He was as confounding as her feelings, yet he felt like the negative to her positive. She could practically see the electrical lines that pulled her to him. She looked at Noah, who had no idea what was really going on in her head. She felt safe and comfortable with him but no pull. Her other secrets suddenly didn't seem big at all.

"Not only are animals, and reptiles I might add, communicating with me but I keep experiencing being hurt," Sloane met Noah's eyes again and he nodded for her to continue, "like being beaten, hurt. But when I come out of it, I'm fine, at least physically. And I keep dreaming about a little boy. Someone keeps hurting him, Noah."

Tears started to well up. "I think I'm supposed to help him but I don't know where he is."

Noah looked away as she blotted the tears.

"Have you told Liam?" he finally asked. Sloane shook her head and heaved out a loud sigh. Noah frowned. "I'm not going to ask why but you must know that I report to him."

Sloane sat stunned for a moment. The thought had never crossed her mind. She had completely forgotten that Liam and Noah were a team. No 'I' in team as they say. Noah breathed out a long 'oh' and stared at the table before speaking.

"Well, I'm going to ask then. Why don't you want to tell him?"

Sloane thought about it. She ran through a dozen reasons that didn't make sense. The only one that did was the burn in her stomach area. She pursed her lips and stared briefly at the cheating man, catching a glimpse of a thought before turning back to Noah.

"You're more approachable then he is," she answered honestly. Noah smiled.

"That I can understand," he said, his warmth and calm like a cloud of sunlight. "He's what we call an old timer. He's gone up against things that some of us have only heard about; big, nasty, scary things. He's one of the bravest and most courageous people I know."

Sloane sat dumbfounded. That was not what she was expecting to hear at all.

"You can tell him," she said. He smiled broadly and patted her hand.

As they got up to leave, Noah tossed some money on the table for the coffees. When she started past the suited man something made her stop. She gently touched his arm. He turned, red and swollen eyes met hers.

"Death is never the answer," she whispered.

"Honesty is." The man pulled back and stared. Sloane gave a small smile and walked out of the restaurant.

The next stop was just a couple of blocks down the road, another family diner, this one called The Barn. Sloane had been to this one and since they only had coffee at the last place, she was betting on lunch. The restaurant had a horseshoe shaped bar in the center and seating off to the sides, making the main entry a bit harder to watch. Noah brought her over to the far left side of the bar with the largest view of the room. He sat to her left leaving the spot to her right empty. She had several rows of booths and tables behind her and to her right. On the other side of the bar were more tables and booths. She couldn't see all of them but certainly enough for their purposes.

Noah excused himself to the little boy's room while Sloane scoured the menu and decided on breakfast. Breakfast was good any time of day and if she recalled correctly, this place made awesome hash browns. When Noah returned, she ordered. Her lip curled slightly as he too ordered breakfast. Once the server had left them, Noah started pointing out people around them for her to evaluate. He scribbled notes as she went.

She was halfway through her meal when two guys wearing green hospital uniforms came in. Sloane put her fork down and stared. One of them was a light yellow, a cheerful fellow. The other wasn't. He was a bilious green. Noah's broad shoulder pressed gently into hers.

"What is it?" he asked, the deep gentle sound bringing her back to present time. She noticed her lowered fork and blinked the daze from her eyes. She turned a frown toward Noah and then back to the guys who were conveniently being seated at a booth on her right, several rows down.

"The one facing us is a light yellow. He's a cheerful guy at the moment. The other is different story. What's weird is I don't see that color very often."

"What color is it?"

" It's a sickly yellow-green."

"What does it mean?"

"I want to say, it's - numb. Or something. Like he has no feelings. I would bet that if you went to talk to him and the subject started to get heavy, he would change it in a heartbeat. Like it wouldn't compute."

"Hm. What makes you think that?"

Sloane was looking at her plate by now. She turned and met Noah's curious golden eyes. She knew emotion was washing over her face in waves and she tried to keep them at bay.

"Because for the last five years or so my mother has had the same hue."

Noah's chin lifted briefly in understanding. It was enough. She felt a tear start down her face and quickly brushed it away. Grabbing a napkin and blotting beneath each eye, she took in deep breathes to regain control. Noah must think her quite a wuss.

"I take it green-yellow is a very bad thing," Noah said softly. Sloane nodded. She looked back at the booth. The two men were placing their order. The bilious hue never changed. No emotion, no cares or conscience, like they were non-people. Goosebumps rolled down her arms at the thought. She may have been miserable but at least she could feel. Noah pushed his plate away and stood.

"Come on, let's get out of here," he said. Sloane didn't have to be asked twice. They hadn't quite hit their time quota so it was decent of him to let her escape. She climbed into his jeep with relief and waited as he walked slowly, texting his way to the driver's side.

Too soon he pulled up to their next destination. Sloane was surprised to see that it was an outdoor ice cream place. She slid from the jeep and waited for Noah. When he didn't get out, she opened the door with a quizzical look.

"Just a drop off," Noah told her as he pointed to a familiar redhead leaning against a black motorcycle at the side of the shop.

"Oh," she breathed out. "See you later then. Thanks, Noah." She gave a quick wave and strolled over to Liam.

Chapter 28

"Good behavior prize for you," he said as he waved his hand with a flourish toward the ice cream shop and gave her a provocative smile. Sloane made a disgusted noise and shook her head.

"What, you don't like ice cream?"

"Of course, I do. Who doesn't?"

"My sentiments exactly." They each ordered a chocolate cone, which of course Liam paid for, and then sat at an umbrella covered picnic bench across from each other and munched away in silence. Sloane managed to be a complete piglet and finish hers first.

"So, you ever going to tell me what you're all about or are you just going to drag me around and stuff food into me until I'm so fat that you'll be able to keep me locked away somewhere to identify feelings for you?"

Liam laughed, it's resonance started a purring orchestra in Sloane's throat. Sloane was so surprised she sucked in air and gave a loud hiccup. A barrage of laughter ensued and tears streamed down Sloane's face. Liam not to such an extreme but she was glad to see he was more relaxed than usual.

"That's not exactly what I had in mind," he finally said. He waited for a moment, gazing into her eyes. She sobered immediately, feeling his scrutiny dig into her soul, igniting the damned hormones and making her uncomfortable as hell.

"So I'm not as approachable as Noah, huh?" he smiled. He was trying to make her comfortable and it wasn't working. Sloane looked away.

"Why is it that when I'm with other Gray One's I feel like I'm wrapped in a warm blanket next to a fire but when I'm with you, I don't?" she blurted out before the thought processed. She instantly turned red.

Glancing at him, she couldn't grasp whatever crossed Liam's face. He closed his eyes briefly and sighed. When he opened them a warm breeze fluttered around her, lifting her hair and caressing her skin like a gentle massage. She felt a hazy calm urging her to sleep and then abruptly, it was gone.

"Like that?" his deep voice startled her from the fog. She nodded, speechless for once.

"I see no reason to sugarcoat reality around you, Sloane."

Her eyes narrowed, "But you do it almost naturally around everyone else, don't you?" He nodded and finished the last bite of his cone. Sloane was unsuccessfully sorting out her confusion when he spoke again.

"I need to ask you something," Liam said as he folded his hands together.

Sloane's eyebrows raised, her heart started

pumping just a little bit faster. "What?"

"Do you take any medications?"

Sloane gave him a disgusted look. "No. Not that it's any of your business." Doubts crept into her mind. "Are you insinuating that I should be?" she asked softly.

"Not at all. I thought that might be the case. Now I need tell you something and you're probably not going to like it."

Sloane cocked her head and looked at him through slitted eyes. Her heart wasn't calming any.

"Remember the spell casting?" he asked. Sloane nodded.

"Remember the bloodletting?"

"Yes."

"I took the towel when I left."

Sloane was angry and creeped out at the same time. "What? I searched everywhere for that thing. Why would you take it? That's just weird!"

"I had your blood tested." Liam's face was stone.

"My blood? For what?"

"Sloane, someone's been drugging you."

Sloane's face went from shock to anger to fear in the flap of a hummingbird's wing.

"Why?" she whispered while she stared at her hands resting on the table. "Why would someone do that? Who?"

One of Liam's hands slid into view and covered her own.

"I have no idea. I only know what I found," he

said tenderly.

"How did you know to even look?" she asked as tears sprang into her eyes. She pulled a hand up to wipe them away and felt him squeeze the other.

"Call it a hunch," he said as he pulled away awkwardly. Sloane finally met his eyes.

"Do you know what it is?"

Liam nodded, "It's a psychotropic drug, an antidepressant."

"Antidepressant?" Sloane spat. "Well, it obviously didn't fucking work."

Stone face was back again. "They're supposed to treat schizophrenia, hallucinations and delusions. Not only do they not actually work but they have side effects that can be devastating. From what the doc can tell, you were given a dose about a week ago. There were only traces left when we did the spell cast."

"God. I cannot believe someone would do that. Who the hell would do that?" Sloane lamented.

"I don't know, Sloane, but you're going to want to take a good look at whoever you're hanging around." He paused before adding, "And it's not me."

Sloane rolled her eyes at him and gave him a joyless smile. "Well, that's good to know."

They sat silent for a few minutes, Sloane staring at the table and Liam watching her. Her eyes hurt and she worked like hell not to break down in front of him. A very light wave of peace soothed over her. She looked up and met his eyes. He didn't move, just watched her back. Sloane gave a small laugh.

"Thanks."

He tipped his head ever so slightly and spoke gently.

"Tell me about the visions."

Sloane sighed in resignation and told him. Liam listened intently, his eyes never leaving her face while hers looked at everything else. She was afraid of the disbelief she might see in his face. When she finished, the only sounds were the cars zipping by and a family chatting noisily several tables behind her. She finally looked up and braved his gaze. It was solid, bordering on menacing. Before Sloane could regret confiding in him he spoke.

"I told you once, Sloane Jacobs, and I will tell you again. There is nothing wrong with you."

Sloane covered her face with her hands and exploded into sobs. Liam moved in beside her and placed a stiff arm around her shoulders. Sloane turned into him and cried into his chest until there was nothing left. A hand full of napkins appeared next to her and she wiped down her face while she waited for her breathing to return to normal. After a deep exhale, she pulled away and laughed at herself. Liam stayed quiet and kept still while she pulled herself together.

"Ok, what now?" she asked him.

"We'll help you find him," Liam said. "Now are you ready for something a bit bigger than haunting restaurants?"

"I think so, presuming they don't all have a disgusting green hue."

"I can't make any guarantees on that. I think you can handle it though. One more request," Liam gave her that charming smile that kept melting her heart. Her eyes narrowed. He must know what that look does to a woman she thought.

"What?" she asked scowling.

"Would you mind terribly, dressing like a prostitute?"

Chapter 29

"I know you're going to want to ask but please don't," Sloane said after Nia answered the phone.

"Ooooh. This sounds interesting."

"Yes and no. But I *really* can't talk about it. I need to borrow an outfit."

"Even more interesting. What kind? Evening wear? I've got a really nice red dress that would look smashing on you."

"Slut wear?" Sloane mumbled.

"I did not just hear you say slut wear. You called me for slut wear?"

"Um. Yes."

Nia laughed. "But of course! Come over in an hour. I think I have just the thing!"

Sloane hung up and sunk into her chair. *This had better be worth it.*

Chapter 30

Verity had gotten in way over her head. Way over. Somewhere along the line she had decided that she wanted adventure in her life. But not like this. A nurse's degree under her belt, she wanted to help people. She had never been very happy except when she was helping.

Finishing off the application of thick black eyeliner, she stared at her reflection in her small compact. The eyeliner made her green eyes brighter and rounder. The shiny clear lip gloss was gaudy. She enjoyed the dark yet sparkly look. Right now she would be happy being someone else entirely and looking completely boring. Checking that her dyed black hair wasn't too messy she looked at the building again, its five stories casting a shadow that stretched across her pale skin and made her shiver inside. She sat in her car scared to death to go inside.

Here was another day that she had to put on her 'happy' face, show up like a good girl and do her job. They thought she was blind and mindlessly doing their bidding. Only she wasn't mindless. Their tricks, drugs and hypnotism, they didn't work on her and she wished they had. She lied when they checked to make sure she had 'forgotten' her visits to the floors below the building. But she hadn't. She knew what they were doing and there was nothing she could do about it without finding herself in a cell. Or worse.

Stepping out of her little silver four-door she grabbed her lunch bag and headed to the main entrance. It had been three months. She had wanted this job so bad, thought she would be doing such a world of good. Now Verity was trying to figure out a way to leave without catching much attention. She entered the reception area, small but elegantly decorated and waved to Myra behind the desk.

Myra was clueless. Their tricks either worked on her or she never needed to know anything that was worth brain washing her. Either way, Verity thought she was okay. The reception area was a small rectangle with the reception desk to the left and six standard cushioned chairs and a side table with magazines piled on it to the right. Ads covered the walls promoting various 'medicines' to cure depression, handle asthma or stop someone from being a shopaholic. *Seriously?!* Verity thought.

To the right of the reception desk was the door to the inner sanctum. Verity paused to punch in her code at the security panel. She deliberately stopped herself from rolling her eyes at the sign posted above it: *Johnson Mental Health Associates - Where mental health is our priority.* She didn't need the security camera in the corner picking up any of her true feelings.

Verity didn't know whose mental health these people were concerned about, but it certainly wasn't the victims imprisoned in the lower floors. The ones that she, Miss Verity Applebee, got to care for.

Making her way to the hidden elevator on automatic, Verity thought hard about how she was going to get herself out of this mess. Her parents were proud that she was working at such a prestigious facility and would definitely not believe her if she told them the truth. There was an interesting group that she had heard about that took down mental health practitioners that committed malpractice, but she would have to get evidence and that would be difficult. Moving out of state would be her best bet, but she'd have to put in a resignation without seeming like she knew anything.

After taking one long hallway to the right and another to the left, Verity arrived at the locked room where the elevator was hidden. George was standing guard. It was always old George or young, hot lookin' Malka who had a really cool accent. Neither of them ever entered the closet, just logged people in and out, storing their personal items in lockers next to the door before entry. Cell phones, cameras and anything else that you might normally have glued to your hip were not allowed past. One of the guards was always on duty.

Verity handed over her purse. There wasn't anything in there that she would ever need *down there*. Not that she was allowed to have anything anyway, she thought. George stuck her purse into a locker, closed it with a bang and started to unlock the door.

"Your bag is in the number three locker today, Miss Applebee," he said as he turned around, holding the door for her.

"Thanks, George." She smiled at him. He was a nice old guy.

"Off you go then. Have a good day."

"Thanks again. You too." She turned away from him and went through the door as he turned, she knew, to scribble her name onto a clipboard. As usual the closet was empty except for the elevator door. Verity hit the down button and waited.

This was where her job got challenging. From the time she entered the elevator to the time she left for the day, she was supposed to forget anything that happened that was illegal, strange, or really friggin messed up, which meant basically everything. She never did, she just had to make them think she did.

During her first two weeks she had been grooved in on the upper floors. That hadn't been much fun, it was a mental health hospital after all, but it wasn't horrible either. Someone must have seen some potential because after that first two weeks Dr. J brought her down to Level A, one floor below ground level, and attempted to brainwash her with drugs and hypnotism. He had told her that any time she came to the lower levels she wouldn't recall anything except that she had helped normal people with normal health care needs and that she would not recall anything out of the ordinary. The problem was that drugs had never worked well on her. Cursed with enduring PMS and headaches with little relief, now she had come to find that hypnotism didn't work either. Verity had been too scared to do anything but nod like she understood and would obey. Forced to judge what she should and shouldn't see she had been working on covering herself ever since.

The doors slid open with a hush and Verity stepped out. This floor, Level B they called it, had a small kitchen, laundry and several storage areas. Her job was to load up a cart of meals, bring it to Level C and deliver them. Occasionally someone needed help eating. If she noticed a bed sheet needed to be traded out or if the victim needed fresh clothes she would help. It was like caring for people in an old folk's home except for one major detail. It wasn't who she was looking after, but what. Verity loaded up her cart with eight meals, the number of guests she had at last count plus two for any new additions, and headed back to the elevator.

At Level C she stepped into her own personal hell.

Heading toward the hallway she listened to the silence of the ward. It was more like a graveyard than a place for the living. Verity liked to work her way down the hall from one side to the other so she could hightail it out of there when she was done. She had finally stopped feeling like throwing up every time she walked down the hall, but she still felt sick. It always smelled like crap, vomit and bleach.

At first glance it looked like any hallway in a hospital; rooms, one after the other, with windows so you could observe the patients. The first difference was the doors. There weren't any per se. Instead there were sliding iron bars like in a prison. Once unlocked, the bars slid into the side of the wall. They seemed to work well to keep those in, *in*. There was an emergency lever near the elevator that she was pretty sure would automatically open all the doors at once. It was protected by a glass case. Verity wondered who would be suicidal enough to use it.

The second difference was that each room had its own stainless-steel toilet and sink just like a prison. She was glad she didn't clean the cells. That was Grodon's job and she was pretty sure he only had about two brain cells because the work didn't seem to bother him in the slightest.

The last major difference was the inhabitants.

Rolling her cart to the first room Verity looked through the bars.

"Hey there," she said to him. Probably in his twenties he would be considered normal looking, until you saw the scales on his legs. They ran from his ankles all the way up to his privates. At least Verity figured they must. He always had on running shorts. The scales disappeared beneath the fabric then reappeared briefly stopping just below his belly button. He only wore those shorts. He didn't seem to have a scrap of fat on him and he was darkly tanned, like he'd lived in the sun most of his life. He had a room heater, unlike anyone else, and it seemed to keep his temperature at some level that he liked because he basked almost naked.

He stared at her without emotion, his small blue eyes burning her skin. He was lazy so she didn't have to worry much about him, which worked for her just fine. She slid his tray through a narrow opening under the window, a lot like a mailbox slot, and it rested on a small ledge inside the cell where he could get to it whenever he was good and ready. She would change his bed sheets on Monday if he didn't need it sooner. It scared her to go in with him, but he barely moved and she didn't think the doctors would tell her to go in if it would hurt her. She hoped.

"Enjoy," she said in a monotone. Trying to have no emotion was what got her through the day. He didn't say anything back, he never did. She pushed the cart down the hall and looked through the next door; the cell was empty. Verity glanced across the hall and saw that room was also empty. Good, she thought smugly until she started walking again and remembered what was next. Taking a deep cleansing breath, she stopped at the next window. It didn't help. He was still there. Her mouth turned down and she choked back a sob. Even though she tried to be emotionless it didn't always work.

He was sitting on the bed, his legs too short to reach the ground and she could see the glimmer of half dried tears streaking down his dirty face. She pegged him to be about six and she could easily guess why he had ended up here.

His skin was so translucent that at times you could see the muscles and tissue beneath. His fine hair was a silvery blond and he almost sparkled. Soft and slightly pudgy, but not fat Verity couldn't help but want to scoop him into her arms and tell him everything would be okay.

But then she'd be lying.

He wouldn't let her near anyway. As soon as she unlocked the door, which was oddly covered with barbed chicken wire, he jumped up and bolted to his usual hiding spot under the sink. She could see him clearly beneath the sink but it somehow seemed to make him feel safer.

"Hi there little one," Verity said gently as she pulled the door shut behind her. He stayed huddled under the sink. She pulled his bed sheets off, as she did every day. She wanted to clean him up, but since she couldn't get near him she made sure he had a clean bed to sleep in. He didn't say anything. It was not a very talkative crowd down on Level C.

When she was done she left the cell and locked the door behind her. She put his food dish through the slot and looked at him. He looked back with his strange iridescent eyes.

"I'll see you tomorrow, kiddo. Maybe then you'll let me help you get cleaned up." She smiled and moved away with her cart, wiping away the stray tear when she was out of his sight.

The next cell was almost as bad but in a

different way. A child size swimming pool had been tossed in the cell and that was where Verity found the next victim every time she came in. Grodon must clean out the water each day because it never seemed to get too dingy. In it was a full size pseudo-woman with webbed hands and feet and two small holes where a nose would normally be found. She had a slit for a mouth and gills starting below her ears and running down to the shoulder. Her taut skin had a grayish green tinge. Despite the strange fish food looking stuff Verity left there twice a day, she looked like she was starving to death. Her body was curled up as tight as she could get it keeping as much under water as possible. Her head was always submerged but even so Verity could feel the hate emanating from the big round eyes that stared out from the water. They bore into her while she stood looking through the window. Verity looked away and quickly put the tray through the slot. That one creeped her out.

The cell across from fish lady was empty, Verity saw. The cell after was also empty but the cell across from that was occupied. Henry lay on the bed, hands behind his head, legs stretched out and ankles crossed. Henry was an older man, perhaps sixty. Almost bald, he had just a white and brown tuft left on the top of his head. His skin was barely wrinkled and he looked strong and healthy, as though he had taken good care of himself his whole life. He had one green eye and one brown and he was the only one in the cells that ever talked with her. He was also the only one whose presence there didn't make any sense.

"Hi, Henry. How are you today?" Verity smiled through the door at him. He smiled back and sat up, swinging his long legs off the bed.

"I am alive, my dear. And you?"

"Well said, Henry. I'm alive."

"Alas, you are also free." He pulled his glasses off and proceeded to wipe them with the bottom of his white tee shirt.

"I s'pose so," Verity mumbled. "I s'pose so."

"Their brainwashing didn't work with you, did it?" His words made Verity stand stiff. "Don't worry, my dear. Your secret is safe with me."

Verity just looked at him. She hadn't known him long enough to know if he was trustworthy. She also didn't know what happened to the others that were there yesterday. One day someone was in a cell, the next day they were gone. It didn't bode well so she didn't answer him and just put his food through the slot. Before she rolled the cart forward to check the remaining cells, she went to the door and leaned her forehead against the bars.

"I hope you make it out of here okay, Henry," she said softly. Henry looked at her with a sad smile.

"I hope so too, my dear. I hope so too."

Chapter 31

Walking down the dark, seedy strip of Fort Harrison Avenue in high heels that kept getting stuck in pavement cracks wasn't Sloane's idea of a good time. *He* seemed to be enjoying it. A lot. Of course, he didn't have to wear these torture devices someone laughingly called shoes.

Nia had come up with an outfit that had raised questions which she coyly avoided. A black suede mini-skirt barely covered Sloane's ass but showed off the fishnets that Liam had shown up with earlier that evening. A deep red corset top completed the ensemble.

Her generous bosom, which was usually well covered, spilled out more than was generally acceptable and definitely more than she was comfortable with. Liam had encouraged her to cake on make-up; smoky eyes and bright red lips. It was the hair she really threw a fit over, but a gallon of hair spray later and Liam was finally satisfied.

Now they strolled along the dimly lit street, Liam dressed all in black down to a black beanie to cover his shock of hair. He asked her to walk a step behind him, which was highly annoying. Some kind of pimp thing she guessed, seeing as how that's what he was supposed to be. Or maybe it was a Liam thing. Was she supposed to be his trick she wondered? Liam said that he needed her as part of his disguise, yes, but that he also needed her to read someone for him.

It was exciting in a weird, scary kind of way. She tried to walk like she imagined a tramp would and with the exception of the cracks in the pavement she thought she was doing pretty well. They were just passing a particularly sleazy, hot pink motel when Liam stopped suddenly and turned to her. With one hand on each of her upper arms he lifted her without even a grunt and she found herself shoved into a hedge. The tall bushes grabbed her hair and pulled at her clothes. Liam somehow squeezed in front her.

"Listen," his whisper was a command. Sloane strained to hear something besides the thrumming in her chest. She wasn't sure if her heart pounded from excitement or his proximity, less than an inch away. She looked at him and lifted both shoulders hoping he read *'I have no idea what you're talking about'* into it. She didn't hear a damn thing save some TV show from one of the motel rooms. Without acknowledgment he cocked his head toward the motel and stared into the brush above her head, listening intently.

Sloane's view was his neck. She tried not to look at it but she didn't have a lot of room to move around. She could smell him too, a light musky smell mixed with the earthy scents around them. *Yum.*

A door opened somewhere beyond them.

Then Sloane did hear something, a gruff voice.

"See ya later, baby." The door closed and footsteps fell just on the other side of the hedge. Liam lifted his head and took in a deep breath before grabbing her hand and stepping out, pulling her with him.

He pulled her close to him with one arm and touched her cheek with his free hand. She froze in the embrace. She wanted to say something but couldn't. The footsteps were suddenly loud and someone rounded the hedge, almost running into them.

The guy snickered when he saw them. Sloane closed her mouth slowly and looked at him wide-eyed. Liam moved gently, still holding her close in ownership. He took the hand that had been touching her cheek and brought it to his mouth. A dark smear of blood caught her eye and she realized one of the branches must have cut her face. How convenient. She glanced at the guy's disgusting smile. The man watched Liam with great interest as Liam put his finger into his mouth and sucked the blood from it.

"Hot, man," Sleazeman said. "Maybe I take a try with her some time."

"Maybe," Liam said in a sultry voice that made Sloane pull her head back slightly and stare up at him. His arm was still holding her snug.

"Does she kiss back, man?" the man asked as he stared at her like a long-lost treasure, "Most of them don't but them that does are *special*."

Liam looked down at Sloane. His face showed

nothing but his eyes searched hers deeply. She became even more aware of his body, the solid warmth and hard muscles. His hand on her neck squeezed ever so slightly. Sloane realized he was asking permission.

She saw concern in Liam's eyes, his hesitation, but it was the hunger, the need that emanated from him that electrified the very air surrounding them. Raw energy coursed through her veins and overwhelmed her core, reaching out to touch the tips of her fingers and toes. Her hand glided to his face on their own and she felt sparks from the heat of his skin touching her fingertips. Only seconds had passed before she blinked hard in acceptance.

Liam's eyes drank her in as he brought his head down, lips close. His breath, soft and warm, tickled her chin and her lips buzzed with anticipation. He just brushed her lips, still hesitant. Sloane's hand eased up his neck into his hair all control lost. Feeling the softness of his hair, she closed her eyes and pushed him down to her. His arms tensed and then pulled her to him, his lips eager and hot. Fire exploded from Sloane's heart and shot into her head making every part of her body sensitive with need. Liam's hand buried into her hair as his tongue teased and explored her lips.

Sloane's tightened her arms around him, his heart beat against her chest screaming to melt into her own.

A sensual dream. Sloane found herself bodiless, her very soul airborne, Liam's essence wrapped around and through her like twine. She felt him there moving without time and space, together they were a forgotten song.

As soon as she saw it she was slammed back into her body. They pulled away from one another, breathless, eyes wide. His shock mirrored her own. Sloane's lips tingled with sensation. She could feel his breath hot and consuming, heavy and intoxicating on her face and his chest thundered against hers. God, she wanted more.

His face went blank then, all emotion wiped clean. He slowly moved away to look at their forgotten audience. The blood that had been flying through her veins started prickling, goose bumps covering her flesh.

Liam's voice was deep and raw when he spoke. "We'll see you around, eh?"

The man looked surprised and impressed. "Sure, man. This my stomping ground. I like to try out the newbies. Heck ya."

Slimebag walked around them and continued down the street, looking back just once. Sloane relaxed a little. She hadn't realized that she had tensed up so much. Liam leaned down close, she felt his breath on her cheek, and whispered, "What did you see?"

Sloane hesitated. She wasn't sure if he was asking about the jerk or their kiss. Sloane decided not to go there. She whispered back, "A scumbag."

She didn't hear anything but she could feel the rumble in his chest as he suppressed a laugh.

He whispered again, "You know, I can see almost to your belly button."

"Dickhead," Sloane muttered as she pushed him away. He grinned at her scowl just as a cop car pulled up next to them.

"Is he bothering you, miss?" the cop called to her from his open window. Sloane's heart raced and her ears burned.

"No, no. I'm fine," she said hoping her voice sounded steadier to him than her. Liam stepped slowly over to the car holding some kind of card. The cop looked at it and nodded.

"Have a nice evening," he commented as he drove off. Sloane wanted to see the card but it had already vanished into the depths of Liam's pocket.

"Let's get out of here. We'll talk back at your place," he said. "I've seen what I wanted tonight."

"I'll bet you have," Sloane mumbled. Liam didn't say anything as they started walking back to her car, which was parked down the street in a bit nicer area, but the shit-eating grin on his face said everything. *Bastard.*

Stepping as fast as she could in the confounded outfit, Sloane thought about Sleazebag. How could women even think about doing that? It made her shiver. His hue had disturbed her, a deep red with a splash of pink in it. A back-stabber.

Even that didn't disturb her near as much as the cause of the power streaking haphazardly through her nerves. A different kind of shiver tore down her back right as she mis-stepped and caught her heel in a deep crack.

Before the stumble could turn into the inevitable fall, arms were around her. As soon as she was upright again she pushed him away.

"How the hell do you keep doing that?"

"Doing what?" Liam looked puzzled.

"Moving so damned fast?"

He just shrugged and held out a hand.

"I'm fine, I'm fine," she said just as she realized that the heel was still in the sidewalk. Liam reached down and pocketed it.

"I could carry you." He held out his arms.

"Oh god no, I said I'm fine." She started walking, limping really, leaving him momentarily behind her before he again took his place a step ahead of her. She couldn't see his face and wondered if she had bothered him. Then she remembered that she didn't care and walked just a bit faster. When she was next to him they walked in rhythm and he didn't speed up. She glanced at him and saw a deep frown etched into his ivory face.

They were silent the rest of the way to her car and then to her apartment. As soon as the door closed behind them, Liam turned to her.

"So what did you see?"

"Oh, no. You're going to have to wait now. There is no way I am going to spend another minute in these clothes."

Chapter 32

Liam sat on the loveseat. He didn't like putting his back to the door but he knew he was the scariest thing around at the moment. The Brownie who lived in the tree outside wasn't about to overhear their chat. That pleased him. Nosy little things those Brownies.

He had figured out the chair was her favorite, unfortunately by the strength of her intoxicating scent, and wanted to be cordial. Why he cared or why she got under his skin he didn't understand. He'd lost count of the women he had courted, but that kiss had been cosmic. He cringed at the use of the word, but nothing else came to mind. It was going to drive him crazy, this assignment. He was stuck with her because he had not handled the initial encounter very well and Brick had decided Liam would be the best one to persuade her to help them.

The problem was the pull, he thought. It was like they were magnets. It took every bit of his control and strength to stay away, especially now after that kiss. Just the thought kindled his lips. He had to fight not to jump up and rush to her room. He growled quietly in frustration. He wasn't doing a very good job holding himself together. She was breaking down his carefully set walls like tissue paper, the layers of stone that he'd meticulously built for more than thirty years being broken by a woman. This, going on right in the middle of vanishing Guardians, was enough to make him growl again. Almost.

He tried not to listen to the shower run while he placed his mind in the zone. Sucking all his emotion down into a pocket, he allowed his skin to roil a bit and then harden. Not too much, not wanting to dent the couch with the extra weight, but enough. It felt good. He released it and sprang up to make coffee.

The shower turned off while he was pouring the cream. He put hers on the coffee table and sat back with his, sipping in its luxury. A few moments later she came out in black sweats and a white tee; her wet hair pulled up and clipped haphazardly onto the back of her head. She picked up the coffee, waved it in front of her nose and gave a small moan as she sat down.

That one sound forced half his emotion to come pouring out of its safe little pocket. While she took a moment to drink, he closed his eyes and tried to shove it all back. He'd gotten most of it in when she spoke.

"Now I'll tell you," she said with a sly grin. Keeping his face solid, he raised both eyebrows and waved a hand toward her in answer, not trusting his voice. She made a grumpy face at him.

"So the guy is unusual. I mean, you do see this hue around, just not that much. I guess because most people are actually good people even if they have something shitty going on in their life. This guy's mostly got red in him, which is hatred or strong dislike. Maybe even evil. Not sure how that works," she looked at him and lifted a shoulder, "what's interesting is he also has a little bit of pink color. They're...mixed somehow. It's weird. I don't really know what it means but he's creepy. You get the idea."

Liam nodded at her. He didn't really care about the guy. It had just been a test of her reactions when put in a volatile situation. It just wasn't supposed to have been *that* volatile. When it occurred to him that *he* had been the one tested he made an effort to flow his frustration away.

Back to business. He considered what they knew. The blood in one of the alleys was from about the same time as one of the disappearances but it didn't match anyone they had on file. The syringe that had been found was a very scary thought for anyone, especially a Guardian. The serum it had contained *could* take down a Guardian, as long as they hadn't changed form or hardened their skin.

"I know it's a hard subject to discuss but the green hue you came across, the one that's like..."

"My Mom's," Sloane interrupted. "Yeah, my luck that would be relevant somehow."

"I'm just looking at every possible connection no matter how slim and that's one we need to follow up on."

"Creepy medical guy and my mom, who

frankly has been acting non-human for a few years now, that's pretty creepy."

Something told Liam there was a connection and he needed to it nailed down. He should have them tailed. Berating himself for not having thought of it sooner he realized that was one of the first things he should have done. The mom would be easy. The other guy not as easy, but hopefully it would give some purpose to the crew. He pulled out his phone and sent a text to Brick requesting the detail. He didn't know how much time was left for Joseph, if any. He really should be...

"Earth to Liam," Sloane's voice penetrated his thoughts. He focused on her and tried not to let her see anything in his face. It had been a week now and he had to get his guys out, if they were still alive. He still couldn't believe someone had been able to get through their armor. The Guardians had been unknown and untouchable for so long it was bizarre to think someone knew what they were *and* had figured out how to capture them.

Sloane cleared her throat and got his attention again. He looked at her and really saw her this time.

"Are you still having the dreams?" he asked softly. She nodded, eyes wide so he continued.

"Not today, but I think we need to take a trip around the nearby neighborhoods and see what we pick up."

Sloane nodded thoughtfully at him. He changed the subject.

"Alright, so I'm going to fill you in on a few things to get you in the loop. Not everything of course, but what you should know so you can work with us and hopefully want to." Sloane nodded at him, eyelids dipping as she took a sip of coffee. Of course, he thought, it was almost three in the morning. She must be tired. He had napped earlier and of course didn't need much anyway.

"You know how there's the FBI and CIA?"

"Yes." Sloane drew out the 's'.

"Good. I'm part of a group that's like them, but not. I'd like to invite you to join us. If you decide to, you will receive payment for your services."

"Seriously?"

"Yep."

"Hm, okay. So, what *is* this mysterious group?" Her half smile entertained him briefly and then he pulled it all back inside. Again.

"We're called Guardians. There are roughly ten thousand of us posted all over the world. We originally started off committed to protecting a particular family line that started in the thirteenth century. Since then, both our numbers and their numbers have grown quite a bit. We keep an eye on them and on each other. We've expanded to handling outbreaks protecting everyone as needed but the family always comes first. We're their Guardians and we consider each other brethren. Our set up is better funded and more efficient than the CIA or FBI and we're known by only a handful of people in the top governments. And that is only because being known by *them* keeps them off our back when we're dealing with things."

Sloane was looking at him with a shocked and amused expression. He clenched his jaw so he wouldn't tell her it was true and waited her out.

"That's the first time I've heard you say so much at one time," she said while searching his face. "So, you're like the Knights Templar, but not. What could I add, besides reading hues?"

"That's actually more helpful than you might think. I am afraid that this investigation may have to do with that yellow-green hue you've seen."

Sloane slumped in her chair. "I thought it might." She rubbed her face. "I wish I knew what those colors mean but I haven't figured it out. I keep thinking that they're brainwashed but that seems so ludicrous."

"Actually, there could be something to that." Liam thought about it. It was certainly a possibility.

"It just seems like such a horrible thing to do to someone. I'm surprised it's even legal. Anything that takes away a person's will to do something is off-the-charts fucked up if you ask me."

"I couldn't agree with you more, Sloane. Here's the thing. For eight hundred years, we've been completely under cover. Now, in the last four months we've had three of our Guardians go missing."

"Just gone?"

"With only a spot of blood and a syringe to guide us. We're doing the best we can. They brought in me and a couple others who tend to deal with the more unpleasant things."

"So you're not actually from around here?" Sloane's voice was soft, her eyes more alert.

Liam shook his head. "I'm here on mission. I'll get sent to the next thing when this is over."

"Oh," Sloane whispered. Liam puzzled over the look on her face. He must have misread something.

"Did you know any of the Guardians who went missing?"

Liam nodded.

"I'm sorry. That's awful." Liam acknowledged her with a nod of his chin. "And you want my help to observe people so we can see if the green hue gets us any closer to finding the truth?"

"Yes."

She was quick, he thought, knowing exactly what he was getting at. He was glad he hadn't had to ask. They both fell silent then. Sloane was obviously grinding over whatever she had to, and he was looking at his life in a completely different light. He wanted to help his brethren, to find Joseph and the others and get everything set straight, but now he wasn't sure if he wanted to leave when it was over. Having been in the business for more than his quota, he could change positions. He'd been working special ops for so long, could he tolerate being a standard guard? Could he stay in one place? Or was it time to move on?

He looked at Sloane. She had taken the clip out of her hair and was balled up in the chair staring toward the kitchen. He knew she wasn't seeing it. He watched her absently rub her chin. He wanted to go over and scoop her off the chair and directly into his lap, but it was unfortunately more important to do his job right then. She turned and met his eyes at that moment.

"Well, it's the only right thing to do. You obviously don't have a roster of Aspie's that you can get in whenever you need, do you?"

"Actually we usually do, but they're tied up at the moment."

"And by helping you, I help these others and then when you leave, I'll be on that roster?"

"You're a smart one, Sloane." He gave her a smile. She cocked her head, brows raised.

"Well, let's see. So far, I've identified over a hundred people's feelings, discovered something that might help, and dressed up like a two-bit whore. What's next?"

"It's time to visit some medical facilities. You up for dressing like a nurse?"

"You just love costumes, don't you?"

"Who doesn't?"

Chapter 33

Her own scream left Sloane shaking in bed, wet with sweat. She still felt the remnant of pain in her stomach.

"Oh, god," she choked out. "Oh, no."

Sloane scrambled out of bed and ran to get her phone from the living room. It only rang twice before she heard his voice.

"Liam."

"You have to come. We have to find him *now*."

"Find who?"

"The boy! Liam, please. He's dying."

"Be right there."

And he was gone. Sloane trembled as she pulled on a tee and a pair of sweats. Slipping into her flip flops she headed out the door. Walking quickly, she left the alley and headed north. She was still walking when Liam appeared from the shadows.

"You do realize you're walking through a shady neighborhood at 4 o'clock in the morning?" he asked nonchalantly. Sloane stopped and stared at him. Her mind was whirling in circles.

"Sloane?" he asked and put his hand on her shoulder. She calmed immediately and realized he was right. She was being stupid and she didn't even know where she was going.

"I don't know what to do."

Liam looked down the dark street and she could tell he was thinking about something.

"Whatever it is, I need to hurry. He'll die from what that man did to him if no one helps him," she said.

Liam nodded. "I don't know exactly how it works, but we'll try. Empty your mind and think of the boy. Think about the things you've seen with him. I know it's not comfortable, but try to think of the pain he's feeling and see if you can hone in on him. Like, pick up a locator signal."

Sloane nodded and closed her eyes. She thought of the different times she'd seen him, felt his pain. She remembered his gentle mother trying to help him. It struck like a paddle of nails straight into her stomach. She doubled over and would have hit the cement if Liam hadn't caught her. He pulled her up.

"Don't let it consume you Sloane. Follow it. Which direction is it coming from? Follow the emotion, babe. Not the pain."

Sloane nodded slowly and took a step, one hand still holding her stomach. The pain ebbed and she stopped. Turning around she took two steps. The pain stayed, a dull ache, but the sobbing in her mind was slightly louder. She looked at Liam through wet eyes.

"This way," she whispered. They walked for three blocks before she doubled over again. Liam held her until it passed and she started running.

They were in a rundown neighborhood six blocks from her home. She passed house after house until the soft cries in her head started to quiet. She stopped and turned around. She retread her steps until she heard him screaming in her head.

She stopped and stared at the house. It was hard to tell in the dark, but it looked to be gray and white, the paint peeling and the yard was more dirt than grass. A battered old station wagon was parked in the small driveway.

Sloane shrieked when a bike whisker past them on the street. Her nerves were shredded. Liam went to the front door and knocked heavily three times. It wasn't a moment before the door swung open.

"What do you want?" the man asked. He was at least five inches shorter than Sloane, overweight and covered in scraggly blond hair. His light blue pebble shaped eyes peered up at Liam without fear.

"My girlfriend and I were out for a walk when we heard someone scream. I was just checking to make sure everyone was okay."

"Of course, we're okay, you idiot. Now get lost."

Sloane's jaw dropped when the man's head slammed against the doorjamb and watched incredulously as he slumped to the ground. She looked at Liam, who shrugged.

"He wasn't being cooperative."

Sloane looked at him for just a moment before closing her mouth and pushing past him into the house.

She found the boy in his room, curled up in a ball on the floor. His face wet with tears and blood, one eye was swollen closed. The other widened at her approach. He tried to squirm away but gave up, pain etched into his skin. Sloane placed her hand on his shoulder.

"It's okay, sweetie. I'm here to help you." The boy sighed loudly, and quiet tears ran down his cheeks. Liam appeared next to her closing his phone.

"I've called an ambulance. They'll be here shortly." He leaned in to whisper in Sloane's ear, "His mom's knocked out in the other room. She looks to be in about the same condition."

Sloane nodded as she sat near the boy gently caressing his arm while they waited in silence.

After the ambulance left, taking the boy and his mom to safety, it was time to deal with the police.

They simply told the truth. That is, the part about taking a walk, hearing the scream and Liam decking the guy. The part about Sloane living the kid's nightmare of a life probably wouldn't have gone over well.

Liam flashed his mysterious card and soon after they were back at her apartment.

It was dark except for the dull light shining through the living room window. Sloane closed the door and lifted her hand to flip the light switch. She hit Liam instead, her hand flat on his rib cage. Warmth shot down her arm and she was about to move her hand when something took over. She threw herself at him, wrapped her arms around his waist and hugged him tight.

"Thank you. Thank you. Thank you," she whispered. He was slower, but his arms found their way around her shoulders and pulled her close. His head bowed down and she felt the warmth of his face touch her cheek, his breathe on her ear. It felt like home.

Chapter 34

The curve of her body pressing against his, her scent and the undeniable need to claim her as his own started to take over. His guard started to slip. He knew that when his lips found hers she would greet him like a starved tiger. He imagined her arms leaving his waist to wrap around his neck, one hand running into his hair, her tongue tracing his lips, him biting her bottom lip gently. Liam wanted to push her back into the door, grip her firm behind and lift her to his height. He thought about Sloane's legs laced around his hips, pulling them even closer.

The feel of her pressing into him thawed his heart and seared his flesh.

Liam pulled away, his chest heaving. He lifted his face upward and breathed out.

"You're welcome," he whispered, his voice gruff. "I'll see you tomorrow."

He left, shutting the door softly behind him. Liam cursed himself as he walked back to his condo. He'd almost lost it. He was started to sound like a broken record.

He'd felt her need and knew she wouldn't have hesitated.

Liam cursed some more as he stalked up the

parking garage, the beginnings of sunrise glinting in his hair.

"*This one's off limits, you understand?*" Brick's words echoed around him. Liam's hand went involuntarily to his lips as he recalled their only kiss. He leaned against a car and closed his eyes, reliving her scent, the taste in his mouth.

"Been busy?"

Startled for just a second, Liam slowly opened his eyes and looked at Noah.

"You could say that," he muttered.

Noah patted his shoulder and moved toward his jeep.

"I'm off to pick up bagels for the crew," Noah paused, "Just so you know, Kam and Ryan started a bet going on how long you can keep it in your pants."

Liam growled, "Does everyone know?"

"Hmm. Pretty much." Noah smiled. "The tension's so high, they've got to have someone to fuck with, right?"

"But not to my face apparently."

"Heck no. Everyone knows that after Brick you're next in line in the ass-kicking department. I think they want to keep their asses intact."

Liam crossed his arms and mumbled, "That's just great."

Chapter 35

It was just after lunchtime when Sloane was startled into awareness by tapping on her window. She threw back the covers, pulled a black robe over her naked body and peaked out the window. She searched around for a moment but the only thing she could see was the squirrel in the tree. She waved at it wearily only to freeze in place when the damned thing waved back. She stared at it for a while. It stared back. She wondered briefly why it continued to surprise her. Finally, she let the drape fall back in place and headed to the kitchen, rubbing her face as she went. She stood absently next the coffee maker while it made her drug of choice.

She was about to sit down, java in hand, when someone knocked on the door. She hesitated at first. The knock came again. She slugged over to the door and leaving the chain on, opened it. Liam stood in all his splendor, letting the sun burn her eyes from their sockets.

"What?" she asked, in no mood to be friendly.

"I brought the nurse outfit," Liam said with a smile, holding up a bag.

"I don't care right now, I need my coffee," Sloane barked at him. He put on an offended face but didn't hold it.

"Coffee?"

"Oh, for fuck's sake." Sloane closed the door, took off the chain and opened it. She turned abruptly and went to her chair, curling into it while hugging her mug. Liam came in and closed the door, dropped the bag near the front door and headed to the kitchen. Moments later he arrived in the living room, kicked off his flip-flops and sat on the loveseat, resting his long legs along the length of the seat. He cradled the coffee and drank quietly.

Sloane tried to ignore him while she waited for the coffee to hit her bloodstream. After a while she got another cup. He stayed quiet while she nursed it.

"I had a squirrel wave at me this morning. And it's not the first time. He can talk. Are you sure you still want my help with anything?"

That seemed to get his attention. He pulled his legs off the couch and leaned forward, elbows to knees. "Do animals talk to you much?"

"Sometimes. But I've always really just thought I was nuts."

"Hm. Not necessarily." Liam went back to the kitchen for another cup. Sloane was glad she'd made a full pot.

"Are you saying Aspies can communicate with animals?" she said to the hallway.

Liam came out of the kitchen. "Well, either you can or you're nuts."

"You're a big help. Sometimes I'm not sure if what I see and hear is real or my imagination."

"Put it this way Sloane, we share a planet with many creatures. Who's to say you can't pick up on their intelligence when others can't."

Sloane laughed. "Yesterday that same squirrel told a lizard to bugger off and the lizard actually listened. The intelligence is astounding."

"I didn't specify the levels of intelligence," Liam said as he made a face. Sloane just shook her head at him, surprised at his temporary humanity.

"So what do you want, besides to annoy me endlessly?" she asked.

Liam held up his coffee.

"Using me for my incredible mind and my excellence in coffee brewing. I see how you are," Sloane said as she thought of a thing or two she would suddenly very much like to get used for. She looked at him and was glad he couldn't read her dirty mind. At least she hoped not. He chuckled at her allegations and drained his cup.

"Just wanted to drop that by and couldn't resist the coffee," he gave her a coffee cup salute, "I've got some errands to run and someone to meet tonight at the coffee shop. We can continue working tomorrow if that's O.K. with you."

"Sure, sure. Lunchtime. Wear the outfit. I know."

Liam bowed and left. Sloane felt unusually alone.

Chapter 36

"He's going to the coffee shop tonight," Sloane told her mother before shoving a mouthful of mashed potatoes into her mouth. Clara beamed at her quietly.

"You should meet up with him." Her step-father said casually. Sloane pulled back slightly in surprise. Reagan didn't usually show any sign of interest in her life.

"You think so?" Sloane asked, feeling unsure and curious about another viewpoint. "I was planning to get some work done at home."

"If he's smitten, I'm sure he would love to see you there," he said.

"Oh, yes," her mother agreed, finally speaking.

"I didn't say anything about him being smitten," Sloane said with a frown. "I said there was a hot new Gray...guy in town."

"I'm sure he'd be smitten," Clara spouted effusively.

"I don't know about that..." Sloane started.

"Don't be silly." Reagan smiled and brushed his hand against Clara's cheek.

"Oh, stop." Clara said smiling back.

Sloane raised an eyebrow. "It's not a smitten

thing," she said carefully, "but maybe I'll drop by."

"What time was your friend meeting?" Reagan asked nonchalantly.

"He didn't actually say," she said. He nodded at her but she could tell he wasn't really listening. Reagan must have sensed her looking at him because he gave her his full attention once more. She raised both brows at him, raising her chin slightly.

"Let me get your special protein smoothie," he said.

"No thanks, I'm stuffed."

"But I insist. Your mother does worry, you know."

"You really don't need to. I've been eating so much better lately..."

"But Sloane dear, it's the least I can do." Something odd crossed over his face and she smiled at him, teeth and all.

"I really just don't have the room."

He let his eyes stay on her just a little too long before giving a nonchalant head tilt.

"Well, fine enough. I will leave you girls to chat while I wrap up some work." He leaned down to kiss his wife on the cheek before walking away. Sloane watched him until he disappeared around the corner.

Chapter 37

Slipping into his office, Doctor J closed the door and leaned back on it. He stared at the ceiling without seeing it. So, the Beasts had found Sloane despite his efforts to cover the Devil magic she wielded. He had tried so hard to protect Clara.

He took out his phone.

"Connor," he said smoothly. "I have a job for you and the boys..."

Chapter 38

It wasn't until Sloane pulled out of the driveway and was on her way home that she lost it. Pulling into the parking lot of a 7-Eleven the hyperventilation took over. She sat, heart pounding and lungs screaming for air.

Stop. Stop it! She screamed in her head.

Stop!

She gripped the steering wheel as though it would prevent her from falling into a deep and never-ending chasm.

She had to drop in at the coffee shop now. The thought of Liam was the only thing that calmed her insides and eased her heart.

She knew who had been drugging her.

Chapter 39

It was dark when Liam parked at the coffee shop. He stuck his head in the door and saw Noah waiting with two cups. Noah got up and sauntered outside, handing Liam one.

"Hey, bro," Noah said.

"Hey, man." He hit Noah's outstretched fist with his own. Liam took a sip of his coffee and they started walking to the alley.

"So you think you've found a stray, huh?" Noah asked, making Liam chuckle.

"Could be. Let's see if we gain ourselves another brethren, shall we?" Liam said as they approached the kid halfway down the alley. Even hidden in the shadows Noah and Liam could see him easily. A few feet away Liam pulled a hacky sack out of his pocket and threw it in Liam speed. The kid went for it and caught it, but the force of the throw pushed him backward. The kid managed to stop his hand just before it slammed into the brick wall behind him.

"Geez," the kid said, rubbing his hand. Liam laughed.

"Hey there, man," Liam said amiably. He was looking forward to meeting a newbie. His friends were all trained and he had only met newbies when he was one himself. With those missing it seemed right to be adding help to their ranks.

"Hey," the kid said tentatively. "Do you think you can help me figure out what the heck is going on?"

"I am pretty sure I can help you. What's your name?"

"Andy."

"Good to meet you, Andy. I'm Liam and this here is my friend, Noah." Liam gestured toward Noah to his left. Andy smiled slightly.

"The first thing I want to know," Andy questioned, "is what the hell am I?" Liam smiled and withheld a laugh, air blowing out of his nose in a quiet snort.

"Well, I need to know a bit more before I'm sure. Tell me what has been happening that's got you so worked up."

"Well, I...uh...see better than others, hear better, and I heal. I don't ever break anything," Andy paused tentatively, "and I can change into a shadow." Andy wore his fear and worry openly. Liam placed a hand on his shoulder and looked down at him.

"Andy, all of those things are perfectly normal," Liam said seriously. "They are perfectly normal for a Guardian, known to the transients as 'Phasers', which I gather you figured out." Liam took his hand away and watched as his words sunk in. Andy stood with a thoughtful expression for a moment. He ran his hand over his not completely shaved dark head and looked from Noah to Liam.

"Well, that doesn't really explain very much," he said with a nervous smile lingering at his lips. Liam leaned in and whispered. Andy's eyes went as round as an overfilled beach ball. Noah chuckled, and Liam smiled.

"Well, you sure are taking it well!" Noah said. "I was not as easily swayed."

"After what I've experienced," Andy said earnestly, "I'm willing to believe almost anything as long as it means I'm not crazy."

Liam put an arm around Andy's shoulder. "Well, Andy," he started, "the fun has yet to begin. We need to figure out how to get your folks to let you go train at a boarding school, so you can learn how to use these abilities of yours while supervised and don't call attention to yourself." Andy stiffened slightly under Liam's arm.

"I don't have any family," Andy said carefully. "I'm afraid I've already called attention to myself. I was in an orphanage."

"Oh shit," Liam said quietly. He took his arm from Andy's shoulder and ran it through his hair thoughtfully. "Where are you staying?"

"In an empty warehouse."

"Hmm. We'll have to get you somewhere safe while we figure this out. When was the last time you ate?"

Footsteps sounded from the rear of the alley and Liam turned to see Sloane walking over. She waved and smiled. Liam waved back but was not excited with the timing. Sloane was about eight feet away when tires squealed from the street where she had come from. Alarms went off in Liam's head.

"Watch him!" Liam commanded Noah who quickly stood in front of Andy, backing him into the wall. Liam tossed his cup and moved toward the wall as he roiled his skin and mingled with the shadows of the alley.

He watched as armed men started to pour out of the open van like a broken water main. He neared Sloane. She gawked at the van while backing up against the alley wall. He could smell her fear as he crept up behind her, still sizing up the men at the end of alley.

He touched her shoulder. She startled, banging her head into the wall. Wincing she looked at Liam. He tasted her rising panic. Her peach skin was glowing white in the shadow. Liam gently touched her face for a moment and her eyes widened.

"I'm sorry," he whispered and backed up.

Gray, veined wings erupted from Liam's back, tearing his shirt as he grabbed Sloane and flew straight up. Sloane's fear stifled her scream. She froze in his grasp, staring at him as he transformed mid-flight. He landed on the flat roof two stories above and set her down carefully. She didn't move.

"I'll be back for you," Liam growled. He backed away from her to the edge of the building and stepped off.

Liam landed next to the dozen mixed-bag of men who had interrupted his evening. He met the first three easily, knocking them down with his fists. He dodged, lunging around three more that came at once. A pipe slammed into his jaw and he fell to his left, rolled back up and tasted blood. He heard someone laugh.

"They can bleed," a tall, bulky man said happily and jumped forward, pipe in hand. Liam swerved just in time, throwing a kick behind him to take down a creeper.

Down at the other end of the alley Noah and Andy watched in silence as Liam battled his way through the men. Andy was amazed and disturbed at what he beheld. A faint whistle of wind caught his attention and he turned in time to see a needle pierce Noah's neck. Noah's skin immediately started to roil, but it was the metal clink of the breaking needle that echoed in Andy's ears. Noah looked at him and whispered, "Run."

Andy watched Noah start to topple before he ran toward the north wall of the alley.

Liam turned to check on them just in time to see Andy disappear through the wall. A heavy weight caught him in the side and he went down only to jump up again and take out the bat-wielding assailant. Only five left. One was pulling the downed men back into the van with some semblance of help from a scrawny driver. The other three circled him, their eyes hard and angry.

Liam was done. He threw out a kick, slamming into the one on his left, and then using the momentum landed his fist into the man in front of him, breaking that one's jaw. Rolling across the pavement he jumped up and brought both fists down on the last man's head - the one with the pipe.

Liam didn't bother to look at the damage as he sped to the other end of alley, only to find it empty except for a few late-night coffee drinkers chatting as they walked along the street. Staying in the shadows he took to the sky. He checked the streets for vans only to find that there were at least ten whites vans going in different directions within a six-block radius. He'd been outwitted. Empty silence filled Liam's ears.

The attackers had collected their people and escaped. Liam landed in the whispery shadows of the alley.

"Andy!" Liam yelled. "Noah!" The echo of his gruff voice was his only answer. He pulled his phone from the shredded remains of his jeans, just pockets and waistband now hanging from his muscled gray hips.

"Yeah?" the voice said at the end of the line.

"I lost them," he said, his voice a deep whisper as he fought to push emotion back into its den.

Chapter 40

Cold sweat and misgivings left Andy gasping. After disappearing through the nearest wall, he had found himself in the back room of the coffee shop. He tore up the stairs to watch the scene unfold in the alley from above.

He had watched as Liam took down one man after another with a speed and skill that he had only ever seen in the movies. Andy watched helplessly as men loaded Noah onto a truck while Liam was distracted. Everything clicked into place for Andy. These men *knew* what they were dealing with.

Something fell to the floor with a crash and Andy saw the room for the first time. Half the room was filled with books, the other half, a dingy brown couch and equally neglected love seat. The rest of the room was bare. He glanced down guiltily at his feet where a vase lay in shatters. Dusty, fake wild flowers littered the floor.

A creak of sound brought Andy's head up and he became still. Someone was coming up the stairs. He hurried to the single window in the office and tried unsuccessfully to open it. Feeling the frame carefully and hoping to find the latch in time, his heart filled his throat, making it hard to breathe. When he finally found the latch and flipped it over the window squealed loudly as he pushed it open.

"Who's there?" a deep, angry voice shouted. Andy didn't stay for a chat. He stepped onto the ledge and looked down. He was only on the second floor, he'd done it before, but onto the soft earth, not concrete. *How bad could it be?* He swallowed and jumped.

As Andy fell toward the cement he screamed silently. *A pair of wings would be good now!* The wind rushed past him, tickling his ears and he thought about the stone-like form Liam had taken. He felt his skin tingle. He was almost to the ground. He hit!

And kept going.

He watched his body go feet first through the cement like water through a hole in the roof. His vision blurred as his head started passing through layers of cement, gravel and dirt. Panicking he wondered if he would just keep going or if he would get stuck in the cement. Suddenly his legs were free and then he was falling again.

The smell of sewage hit him as he fell. His stomach recoiled, but he concentrated on being solid. *Be solid, be solid. PLEASE, be solid.*

Crack! He landed with a grunt, his knees buckling only slightly, his hands thrown out for balance. A crack burst from where he landed and continued several feet down the long corridor. He had managed to land on a damp cement walkway with grates every fifty feet or so. He could hear the gurgling and smell the stench of sewage running through the pipes below.

A surprised breath caught in Andy's throat when he realized he was fine. Catching a glimpse of his hands he gasped. He slowly pulled them up to his face, heart thumping behind his eyes and inspected the hard, leathery skin. He flexed them and saw long sharp claws where there should have been fingernails. They moved back and forth making him feel like a puppeteer.

He felt his chest through these new hands, his shirt was stretched almost to the tearing point by the hard muscles and sinew that now bulged beneath. He leaned over to look at his legs. His pants were taut against him. The inseam split at one ankle and ran halfway up his calf exposing more of the leathery, gray skin. Then he saw his shoes. Claws like knives had pushed through where his toes should have been.

Andy blinked and noticed the change in his face. His eyes felt immense and the darkness filtered through them like it was early morning. He blinked again at the revelation of superior vision. Excitement coursed through him. He was some kind of superhero. Though he was eager to learn all about his new capabilities, the stench wafting through his snout brought him to reality. He needed to find Liam. He needed help and there would be time for exploration later. Andy glanced once way and then the other, picked a direction and started to walk. Hoping he could find an exit and get back to Liam before he was gone, his flopping shoes, the running water and the scurry of rodents were his only company.

Chapter 41

The youthful girl sat in her room fuming. Her parents had not let her play at Christy's house today because they'd things to do. What things were more important than playing, she did not know. Well, she wasn't going to let them tell her what to do. She would go herself. After gathering her blanket, a candy bar she had been saving since Halloween, and paper and markers into her pink backpack she snuck out into the hallway. Her parents were in the family room looking over papers and occasionally at the computer. Making her way to the front door, she flipped the deadbolt and waited. No one came running down the hall. She opened the door slowly and slipped through, closing it as softly as possible behind her.

She waited. No one came. No Mom. No Dad. She glanced out into the dark neighborhood and waited just a moment more. Nothing. She could hear the TV blaring from next door. She headed down the walkway and randomly went left, following the sidewalk, determined to get to Christy's.

About five houses down she started to get nervous. After ten she was almost shaking in her shoes. As she started to pass the next house a low growl seeped into her ears like water from a pool. She stopped in her tracks. Savage growls jumped out at her. A glance to her left showed a large German Shepherd just a few feet away, its muzzle protruding from the chain link and dripping with spit. Fear spread like disease and she ran straight across the street, no thought of cars, and dove into a bush. Twigs pulled at her shirt and scratched her skin.

Through the gaps in the bush she could make out the outline of a two-story house next to her, its color blending into the shadows. Something more monstrous then the dog was leaning against the house, its black eyes grilling into hers. She froze, staring, hoping it hadn't seen her but knowing it had. Trapped, eyes wide, her breath started coming in short gasps. Air wasn't quite getting through as she waited for the monster or the dog to get her. As she stared through the darkness, her eyes just starting to go blurry, she laughed softly at herself. It was just a statue. She had seen something like it in a book or somewhere.

She crawled out the back of the bush and peered around it to the street beyond. Something pink in the street light caught her eye and she realized she had dropped her backpack. She looked down the street toward her home. Should she sneak back to the safety of home and parents who would miss her if she was gone? She shifted her gaze the other way. Her shoulders slumped. She really didn't know how to get to Christy's.

Something shuffled in the grass behind her and she went still. Cold filled her veins as she turned her head slowly. The statue was no longer leaning against the house. It was kneeling just a couple of feet away. She stared up at it, her breath short again. It was huge, taller than Dad huge.

Its mouth curled up, exposing long fangs. The young Sloane opened her mouth but before even a squeak could come out, everything went dark.

~~*~~

She knew now. The fear she had relived blew away with a gust of wind. Looking over the flat roof, the dull glow above a stairwell door her only light, she remembered when she had come to after fainting. She had woken up just inside her own front door, her backpack leaning against the wall next to her and the murmur of her parents coming from the family room. She was in one piece and safe.

She had stood up and opened the front door, looking from side to side in the darkness for her new friend. "Hello?" she had called out. When nothing but the crickets answered her whisper, she had taken her backpack to her room and had one of the best night's sleep of her young life. But she wasn't supposed to remember that, was she?

Sloane now found herself standing exactly where Liam had left her. A short brick wall went around the roof, clearly not meant to keep anyone from jumping. The dirt and pigeon droppings told her it didn't get visitors often. No noise came from the alley below. She started to go to the edge when something whispered and landed with a gentle thud behind her. She guessed he didn't have to make any noise and that it had been for her benefit. At least she hoped it was him. She turned to find him directly on the raised stairwell just ten feet from her. She met his dark eyes with her own and they held for a moment in silence. Sloane broke the gaze and ran her eyes over him.

His skin was like a mix of stone and leather. A long gray tail came to a point like an arrow and moved like a cat's in the dim light. Spikes protruded from his back, arms and legs and his wings, now pulled in behind him, towered over his head. They were massive and yet looked like delicate webbing. And his face. The jaws had elongated into a proud snout; dagger sharp teeth hung over his lower lip. Two horns settled neatly between tall, pointed ears and a small red tuft that seemed slightly out of place nestled between the horns. Large eyes like black glass watched her. He was beautiful and frightening at the same time.

He jumped down from his perch to stand before her and started to change his upper half, slowly as if he wanted her to see. His skin shimmered, swirling in shadows of gray and silver.

"Stop," Sloane said softly. The mesmerizing echoes of darkness melted away into the night and he stood tall and grand before her. She gave him a small smile and he cocked his sculptured head at her. Sloane walked slowly over to him. He crouched down for her, one knee on the ground, his arm resting on the other, yet still he looked down at her. She met his bottomless eyes and then took in his crouched figure. Sloane raised her hands and placed them on his cheeks. He bowed his head slightly and closed his eyes, letting her silently run her hands over his face, gently touching his horns, running a finger down one tooth. She touched his loosely hanging arm and was surprised by the obvious shiver that ran up and across his shoulders.

Sloane went behind him and ran a hand across one of his wings. It was like a soft, textured leather and visions of being wrapped up in them flit across her mind. She left the wing and ran a hand down his back and feeling another shudder spread over him she continued down, feeling the hard spikes as she went.

Sloane came back around and touched his knee, pulling away quickly. His eyes opened and stared back. It felt like he could see through to her soul. She gave him a small smile.

"I'm okay, you know," she said. "If I thought I felt safe with you before, I certainly do now." A rush of warm air blew from his nose.

"They took Noah." His voice was a soft thunder.

Tears blinded Sloane and she wiped them away. She looked up only to find that Liam had partially changed; his torso and upper body were smooth and flush. She had always thought he looked flush for other reasons; now she knew how wrong she had been. His lower body was still solid muscle, gray and leathery. It reminded her of a centaur.

"He's not the first to be taken, Sloane. I have to find them," he said gently. She nodded, a stray tear running down her face. Before Liam could say anything more she lunged forward and wrapped her arms around his neck, burying her face just below his ear.

Liam froze for several seconds before slowly bringing his arms up. One hand came to rest on the back of her neck, the other on her lower back. His musky, sweet scent brought a calmness she was certain no other Guardian could produce.

"I need to get you home and find them, Sloane."

She nodded, still buried in his neck, only drawing away long moments later.

Chapter 42

It only took Andy a few minutes to find a manhole. He climbed the ladder to the top only occasionally catching his shoes on the bars. Lifting the cover slowly, he peered into the darkness. A street light down the road gave off a dull light, but thankfully left him in the shadows. No one screamed at him, so Andy shoved the cover aside and climbed out, thankful that his body had returned to normal. He slid the cover back on and started trotting the block back to the ally. The shoes were such a burden that he pulled them off and tossed them into a dumpster on the way.

As he turned the corner into the alley he looked up to the building and caught a glimpse of something in the air. He lost sight of it and stared at the sky for any anomaly. Finding it again, heading east, he ran to follow it glad of the darkness and lack of traffic. The city might be asleep but he was wide-awake. He ran down the alley, down two streets and just caught the mist coalescing on a high balcony of a large condominium. He watched as the lady he had seen earlier in the alley was left on the balcony for just moments as Liam ran inside and then returned with something. They took to the air again almost vanishing into the night, but now that Andy knew what to look for, he could follow easily.

He had stepped on something sharp during his earlier high tailing and blood was dripping from his heel as he ran. He ignored it and ran like his life depended on it, especially since it did.

If he had any breath left Andy would have chuckled when he found himself back in the alley. The swirls of night had landed somewhere just beyond the coffee shop's long building.

Andy caught up to them at the front door of a small apartment. A huge gargoyle stood with the lady, Andy knew it was Liam but it still made him hesitate. He looked at the lady, her face flush from the wind and shiny with dried tears, who seemed unconcerned that she stood next to a gargoyle while she fumbled with keys. Finally, the door opened, and she stepped inside.

"Liam!" Andy called out as softly as he could while running toward them. Liam turned, his skin starting to swirl. It stopped as soon as his eyes met Andy's. He gave him a nod.

"Glad you caught up," he said, the voice so deep and sinister Andy felt a chill run down his back.

Andy closed his eyes and took in a cleansing breath as he reached Liam. He hoped this night was almost over. When he opened his eyes, he found Liam had changed the upper part of his body to his normal human form, the bottom half still beastly. Liam looked over Andy's tattered clothing.

"You changed," Liam commented. Andy nodded. Liam gave him a small smile, "Sorry I wasn't with you."

"It's okay." Andy smiled back sheepishly. He started to say something else when Liam's arm moved with reckless speed, knocking him to the ground.

Shocked, he looked up and watched in horror as Liam's hand went to his neck in surprise. The lady screamed as Liam's legs started to buckle. Andy shot up from the ground, grabbed Liam and pushed him into the apartment. They tumbled onto the living room floor and Andy heard the all too familiar metal snap of a needle.

"Oh my God, oh my God..." the lady kept repeating. She went to her knees and carefully pulled Liam's head into her lap. The broken needle lay on the floor near her knee. Andy jumped up and went to the door. The only light came from a dim streetlight, so he left the door open just inches, lay on the floor and peered out into the night. He willed his skin lightweight and hoped he didn't fall through the floor as he scanned the dark building across the small parking lot.

Two shadows were moving, one streaking toward him and the other heading toward the rear. Andy slammed the front door, flipping the locks before turning back to the lady and Liam. She was brushing the hair out of Liam's lifeless face.

"It's not safe here for us," Andy said to her.

She nodded unhappily. "Back door?" he asked.

She nodded and pointed to the kitchen. Laying Liam's head gently on the floor, she followed Andy as he went through the kitchen.

He found the back door and opened it a few inches to have a quick look. The lady stood behind him, trying to peer around. Across a small alley, just big enough for two people to walk side by side, a small parking lot stretched before another building, closed and dark.

An outside force crashed the door into his shoulder, shoving him hard into the lady. She cried out before he heard a loud thud and silence. The door kept pushing open and a rifle came through, pointed straight at him. Andy did the only thing he knew; he pulled the door open and rushed the dark figure, slamming him to the gravel. He lifted both fists to start pounding but realized the man had stopped moving. Andy rolled off the top of the man, his lungs sucking up air deeply as though he hadn't been breathing. He stumbled to the door and found the girl laying on the kitchen floor holding a dishtowel to her temple, blood dripped from her chin. He started toward her and she waved him away, whispering, "They want you two. Save him, get out of here. I'll be fine."

Andy gave her a long look. "Go!" she yelled at him. Andy ran to the living room, pulled up Liam and tossed him over his shoulder. The weight made him stagger but he caught himself.

It was time to find out a bit more about his skills. Leaving the apartment, he stumbled into the back parking lot.

He heard the flit of another shot taken and twisted slightly, losing his balance, the weight of Liam costing him his normal dexterity. He felt his knee crack on the cement and bellowed out in pain and frustration.

Andy forced himself back up, pain shooting up and down his leg. Swallowing and forcing the pain down he ran haphazardly toward the back of the quiet building. Pulling Liam down slightly and hugging him close, he willed his skin to shadows and squeezed his eyes shut as he hit the wall.

Chapter 43

When Verity arrived at the cells on Wednesday she knew something was up. Scale boy was pacing back and forth in his room like he was trying to remember something. Every now and again he would murmur something inaudible and rub his face. Verity gawked at him. She'd never seen him move, not once. She slid his tray through the slot as he kept pacing away madly.

"Hello," she said through the bars. He stopped for a moment and looked at her. Verity smiled and gave a small wave. He stared for a moment and then started pacing again. His muttering followed her to the little boys' cell. As usual, her heart twisted when she saw him, but this time when she unlocked the door he stayed sitting on the bed. His legs swung back and forth; under the bed, straight out; under the bed, straight out. When she shut the door behind her, he looked her right in the eyes.

"I'm ready now," he said. His voice sounded like soft bells ringing in the distance. It was musical. For a moment Verity just stared, until she remembered herself.

"Ready for what little one?" she asked

smiling, though concern about the sudden activity on Level C rose the hairs on her neck.

"I need to be clean," he said. He wasn't smiling and he wasn't rushing into her arms. He just sat on the bed, swinging his legs, looking at her intensely.

"Excellent." Verity beamed, all else forgotten. She went back out and grabbed a washcloth from her cart. She always kept it stocked with sheets and towels, never knowing when they might come in handy. She soaked the cloth in the sink and knelt by the boy. He didn't bolt, just sat stiffly, looking at her. It was unnerving, but she was glad to finally be able to take care of him.

Gently wiping the grime and dried tears from his face, she told him a story.

"Once there was a beautiful little horse named Sunny. He loved to play. He would run up the hills, run through the springs and shake himself, water flying everywhere," Verity paused when the boy started trembling. He was looking down as she wiped his neck. Going down on her knee she looked into his face.

He was smiling and held back the remaining giggle that had caused his body to tremble. Verity felt her eyes fill and blinked to keep the tears at bay. Standing again, she went back to his neck. They must have dug him out of a hole, she thought.

"So, one day Sunny got lost. The sun was starting to go down and he had run around so much that he couldn't remember which way to get home. He started wandering around not sure what to do when a man jumped out of the bushes and threw a rope around his neck. Sunny went up on two legs and kicked, but the man was strong. He pulled that rope and held little Sunny tight." Verity felt the boy tremble again and she glanced at his face and saw tears.

"Don't cry, little one. It gets better." The boy nodded and watched while she started wiping down his arms. They were as soft as newborn skin and felt almost spongy when she squeezed just slightly.

"So, the man brought Sunny to a barn and he locked him in a stall with water and hay. Sunny was very scared. He backed into the stall as far as he could go and wouldn't let anyone touch him. Then one day a girl brought him an apple. She left it at the front of his stall and went away. Sunny was so hungry for the sweet apple that he ate it all up!"

Verity tickled him just under the arm and he giggled before shoving her away. She started cleaning his other arm.

"The next day the girl brought him another apple. He was so excited that he started eating before she had even left the stable. The next day, again, the girl brought an apple. Sunny ate it right out of her hands. She petted his face and hugged him. The next day..." Verity left the cell to get clean sheets from her cart. She put them on the bed and continued to wipe him down.

"The next day the girl brought an apple again. When Sunny was done eating it she put a rope around his neck and led him out of the barn into a fenced area. She took the rope from him and he ran around and around. But he couldn't leave. The fence was too high. He stopped in the middle of a run and hung his head.

"The girl brought him inside but day after day he wouldn't eat her apples. One day, she took little Sunny out to the fenced area. He went with her, but his head hung low and he just stood next to her. A sound brought his head shooting up and excitement ran through his whole body." Verity paused while she got the dirt out from in between his fingers.

"What was it?" the musical voice asked her.

"It was Sunny's mother. She was standing beyond the fenced area under a huge tree. The girl looked at Sunny and then at his mother. A sad smile appeared on her face as she walked over to the side of the fence. She slowly opened the gate." Verity glanced at the boy. He was staring at her silently, waiting for the rest.

"Sunny ran to the gate but stopped before passing the girl. He looked at her close and watched the tears roll down her face. He nuzzled his nose in her hair. He was thanking her, you see?" The boy nodded.

"And then he ran to his mother. He ran all around her and then they disappeared into the trees. He went home." She knelt by the now mostly clean boy.

"Don't give up yet, little one. You never know what will happen next." The boy nodded at her thoughtfully. Verity started to remove the sheets from the bed and the boy stood and moved away.

When she finished making the bed, he sat back down while she replaced the pillow case. When she was done she leaned in and kissed his forehead. He pulled back in surprise, eyes wide. She smiled.

"I'll see you later on, little one." He nodded at her and started swinging his legs again. She could feel his eyes on her as she continued down the hall. She so badly wanted to take him with her.

When she got to Henry's cell, it was empty. Verity closed her eyes and said a few words of hope to whoever might be listening before starting down to check the remaining four cells, all of which had been empty the day before.

She arrived at the last cell on the left and looked in. For the umpteenth time that day Verity felt emotion stir her heart into a pounding frenzy. This one was a bit different. He was beautiful.

Chapter 44

At first glance Verity felt awe. He was like a sun kissed god with wings of varying shades of gray. They were protruding from between his shoulder blades, draping down on either side of him. Verity realized she had pressed herself against the cell bars, one hand tightly gripping a bar on the side of her face. Coming back to reality, at least she was pretty sure it was reality, Verity started to see what she hadn't wanted to.

He was lying on the bed on his stomach. It looked like he'd just been tossed there, his legs hanging off the far side and one well-muscled arm dangling down on her side. His head was only halfway on the pillow, his curvy mouth hanging ajar just above a puddle of drool.

There was a lot of blood. It was smeared on his face, in his spiky blond hair and on his neck and back.

Verity felt heat rising in her neck and face. She grabbed the key from her cart along with a food tray and towel. Her hand shook with anger as she unlocked the cell door and stepped in. The angelic man didn't move.

Verity pushed her anger down a few notches and walked quickly over to the bedside to lean over and inspect the damage. He was almost naked, wearing just a pair of black boxers with frogs on them. Some type of metal contraption was embedded in his back between his wings. The gash on his head seemed to be mostly healed and she guessed that to be where most of the blood had come from.

Going down on one knee, Verity looked at his face. Although there was dried blood all around his nose, it didn't seem to be broken. They weren't supposed to just dump the victims in here like animals, she thought angrily. At least they hadn't before. They were always mended and bandaged up first. Why was this one...?

Before Verity could finish her thought his hand was around her throat. Her eyes bulged as she unsuccessfully tried to breath. She tried to talk, tell him she was not a bad guy, but the only noise she heard was a faint gurgle.

His grip relaxed slightly, and she grabbed his wrist with both hands as she gulped in air. When Verity could focus on his face again, golden, slitted eyes watched her. They looked tired and pained, but there was a hint of life and strength burning there. The very uncomfortable pressure of his hand still gripping her throat, she tested her voice.

"Please," she managed to whisper, "I can help you."

She continued to meet his eyes, breathing shallowly so she wouldn't choke. Finally, his eyes slid closed, then scrunched in pain. His arm dropped away from her throat and swung back and forth against the bed as if all the life had vanished from it.

Still stunned, Verity sat on the floor and breathed, massaging her throat until his swinging arm came to a stop. She hauled herself up with both arms and touched her throat again. She had never even seen his arm move. Verity cleared her mind and wet the towel she had brought. She spoke to him gently.

"I'm going to clean up your wounds the best I can." No answer.

"Then I'm going to help you get a bit more comfortable." Still no answer.

"Then we'll see if we can get some food into you." She heard a low grunt from him and rolled her eyes. Men and food. A half hour later she was rinsing the bloody towel out in the sink, her back to him.

"Any chance you could get me some pants?"

Verity startled at the softness of his deep voice. She turned slightly to look at him. He had turned his head and met her gaze, his eyes catlike. Verity stared, mesmerized, before finally turning away, ignoring his question for the moment. She hung the towel over the sink before moving to stand over him. She had cleaned all the blood off him. The gash in his head was miraculously healing on its own so no further medical attention had been needed. His back had been another matter and clearly the object of most of his pain. After cleaning up the blood, which he had hissed and moaned throughout, she had looked it over carefully. Without an xray, *or hello, a doctor's degree*, she had no idea how to remove the metal from his back. Even if she had figured it out, doing so would likely cause them both a lot of trouble. So instead, she had smeared a thick layer of anesthetic gel over the area and hoped it would at least help numb the pain.

Once that was taken care of she had helped him stand and been surprised at the five or six inches he had on her. He had looked smaller lying down. He stood with an arm against the wall to hold himself up, his eyes closed and his face set in a grimace. Verity had straightened his bed sheets and rearranged his pillow as quickly as possible. Then, while trying not to gape at his amazingly muscled chest, she helped him settle back down with his head and chest on the pillow so his long wings wouldn't hit the walls. In that position she would also be able to help him eat.

"If I find you clothes they will notice," she finally whispered to him as she knelt at the end of the bed with the food tray. He scowled but she knew he understood.

Verity lifted a spoon of what seemed to be a vegetable broth to his lips and he accepted until the bowl was empty.

"Why are you doing this?" he asked.

Because he was the most beautiful thing she'd ever seen? Because he was like an angel? Because he was a victim and didn't belong here? Verity pursed her lips as she tried to think of a sensible answer. He waited patiently, watching her the whole time.

"It just seemed right," she finally answered. "What's your name anyway?"

"Noah."

"Noah." She repeated it aloud to herself thoughtfully. Then she realized he was looking at her expectantly and she could feel the blush rise in her cheeks.

"I'm Verity."

"Please to meet you, Verity." Her name sounded soft and silky on his tongue. He closed his eyes and lay his head down. Verity cleaned up slowly, not wanting to leave him but knowing she had other things to take care of. She could drag it out no longer and unlocked the cell door to leave.

"Verity." His voice sent a ripple down her spine.

"Yes?" she whispered.

"Thank you." Verity stopped and shook her head in surprise.

"Sure," she answered, like it was no big deal. Verity locked the door and stood for a moment sadly watching him drift off into sleep.

Chapter 45

Every nerve in Sloane's body was snapping and stretching uncomfortably, like she had inhaled espresso, ice cream and chocolate all at once. A sleepless night at Nia's apartment had left her agitated in addition to her worry. When she arrived home there had been no bodies lying around. They were just gone. That only disturbed her more. Sitting in her purple chair, she dropped the cell phone to her lap after leaving yet another message for Liam.

A loud thump on the back window made her jump. She twisted around to look out only to see the squirrel, waving madly and shaking its head. Sloane lifted a weary eyebrow and was about to tell it to get lost when someone knocked on the door.

Hoping it might be Liam she bee lined to the door and swung it open.

"What are you doing here?" she blurted out, then rephrased, "I mean what brings you here?"

She heard a loud screech from the squirrel as her stepfather leaned in and put a hand on her shoulder. "Sloane, I think it's time you came with me." On this last word, she felt the pinch of a needle in her neck. Understanding came crashing down on her just before the day turned to darkness and then there was nothing.

~~*~~

Liam sat straight up, the dizziness hitting him like a set of Rak twins. He felt his stomach clench and quickly lay back down again, pulling his legs up. *Well, I'm not dead.* He realized he was in his own room at the community den. The blinds were drawn but daylight poured in through the open door. His settling stomach made him realize his head was pounding. He grimaced as pain slid through, jarring his temples. *Ow.*

A shadow filled the doorway. Liam glanced over, eyes only so he wouldn't move his head.

"You're awake!" Andy trumpeted and went down on his knees beside the bed.

"Barely," Liam answered bringing his hands up to hold his head. "What happened? And say it softly."

"Sure. Sure," Andy whispered. "After you got nailed, I grabbed you and went out the back door. We went through a building and I brought you here as fast as I could."

Liam took a silent moment to let it filter into his foggy brain.

"Where's Sloane?" he asked and started to sit up despite his head.

"She's fine," Andy whispered, "she's fine. After I dropped you off, I went back, and she had taken her car and left. I don't know where she went, but she got away."

Liam nodded, regretted it and eased back down to the bed. "How did you know to come here?" he asked.

"I followed you, saw you come here, right after the..."

Liam moved his hand in a downward motion, stopping him. "Good job, Andy," he whispered. "And thank you." Andy beamed.

"What do we do now?" Andy asked his face masked with uncertainty.

"I need a bit more time." Liam now knew the meaning of migraine. Andy frowned thoughtfully before speaking.

"I'll bring you something to eat," he said and left the room. Liam fell into a troubled sleep.

When he woke the room was dark. Someone had shut his door but light curled in from the seams. A sandwich was withering on the bedside table. He scrunched his nose at it and sat up slowly, sighing with relief. The pain was finally gone. Standing, the smell of coffee drifted through his senses. He opened the door and headed to the kitchen. As he went through the living room he saw Andy sprawled on the couch, sleeping soundly. A glance at the clock told him it was a couple hours past the witching hour.

In the kitchen Liam just missed running smack into Danni. She fluttered her eyes at him.

"Hey, Liam. Asleep almost a full day, who would've thought."

"Shit." He brushed by her and went straight to the coffee maker.

"Out." Brick's baritone shattered the uneasy

silence away and replaced it with anger. It wrapped itself around Liam's neck. Danni left the room in a huff. Ignoring them both he poured cream into his coffee and finally turned to lean back against the counter top.

"What were you thinking?" Brick's soft tone belied the torrential energy pouring into the kitchen. There was a reason Guardian's had to be in good control of their emotions.

"I did what I thought was the right thing at the time," Liam said before taking a sip. "Noah is trained. There was no reason for me to think that he would be taken. Neither one of us was expecting to be ambushed, and I certainly didn't expect a sniper."

Brick stared at Liam, his fire doused with that bucket of reason. He nodded, a quick chin lift, and crossed his arms over his chest, easily twice the width of Liam.

"What about the girl?" he finally asked.

"I wasn't really paying attention when Andy hauled me home," Liam backlashed. "I guess she's home now, probably worried as hell."

"She's not." Brick stared at him. Liam lowered his coffee, eyes narrowing.

"What do you mean?"

"We went to get her. She's not there. She had you fooled."

Liam's eyes narrowed. "I don't believe it."

"Go see for yourself. If you find her, bring her here."

"You actually think she had something to do with this?"

Brick sighed. "I know you don't want to see it, Liam, but she was the only other person who knew you would be in that alley. Now she's missing. That doesn't bode well."

"You don't know her, Brick. I don't believe it. But I will be cautious. I should never have been on that assignment, Brick."

"Put a clamp on it. So, you bonded. It happens," Brick waved his arm in the air like he was brushing away a mosquito. "But she's attached to all this and we need to figure out how. I've got Ryan and Kam doing background checks on her relatives. You finish repairing yourself and see if you can find her in the morning."

Liam stood motionless, staring at the empty space where Brick had been. Shock was not even close to how he felt. He scanned back over the last few weeks and understanding dawned on him like a tidal wave in the desert. He turned, put down his coffee cup and placed both hands on the counter. He bowed his head as flashes of memory whirled through his mind.

The connection he had felt the moment he laid eyes on her. The feeling of being engulfed within her during their kiss, and the pull he couldn't seem to escape.

A soft touch on his back brought him to present time. He turned and grabbed a wrist. His eyes met Danni's. She glowed and bent her head downward, her eyes yet gazing up at him.

"Why, Liam..." she whispered seductively. He dropped her hand like it was acid.

"Leave me alone, Danni," he said evenly. She raised an unbelieving eyebrow. Liam picked up his coffee and gave her a pained look.

"I seem to be bonded," he said before leaving the kitchen.

Andy was awake in the living room. They nodded at each other silently. Andy looked at him expectantly. Liam shrugged and went to his room to await the daylight.

Chapter 46

When Liam arrived at Sloane's apartment there wasn't a single light on inside. He knocked on the door but after no answer, he tried the handle and it opened easily.

"Sloane?" he said into the darkness. He could see just fine but he flipped the switch by the door anyway. The lamp near her purple chair came on emitting a glow that would normally be warm but just left him feeling empty. He went to the kitchen first. The gift basket had long been emptied and put away. Nothing seemed amiss. As he strode through the living room toward her room he glanced over it, noticing nothing unusual.

When he reached the bedroom, her scent overpowered him. He stopped in the doorway and breathed in deeply. Leaning against the doorframe, her smell mixed with his growing fear that something wasn't right and it made him almost dizzy.

He looked over her room but since this was his first visit into it, he couldn't really say if it was normal for the bed to be unmade or the clothes strewn around. The rest of her house was spotless.

Liam suddenly wished that he had disobeyed orders and grabbed her when he had a chance. He could think of a few things he would have done with her in that room.

After checking her bathroom and finding nothing, save a bath pillow in the sink, he went to leave when something familiar caught his eye. Sloane's black leather purse sat on the small table near the front door. In all the places they had gone together, she had never been without it.

Chapter 47

"This one's tough, eh, Hal?" Doctor J commented to his assistant who just nodded. "900 volts and still kicking. Amazing. Sooner or later one of these things is going to break and give me the information I want." He used an elbow to hit the intercom button.

"Benny, can you come get the specimen? I need to think up a different tactic this time. Bring me the fish guy. I think I'll work with him for a spell."

Chapter 48

Sloane tried to open her eyes. Dried sleep and tears tore at her lashes. She went to move her hands and found them numb. She tried to lift her feet and couldn't tell if they had moved. She couldn't see, couldn't feel. Panic threaded her nerves. Then she remembered to *feel*. Blind, she focused on relaxing, on feeling the room, see if she could pick up emotions or thoughts of anyone that might be around.

Before she could find anything, she found herself floating on a cloud near the sun, her bikini fitting just right as she lay on the soft powder. Liam was there, smiling and holding a chocolate ice cream out to her in one hand and fish net stockings in the other. The ice cream stayed frozen despite the heat and the black fishnets looked great with her blue bikini. The sun started to move away, pulling Liam with it. Sloane stood and screamed for him as a chill crept up on her, wrapping over her skin like seaweed, forming icicles on her fingers and knees. The cloud split open and she fell into darkness and didn't stop. She just kept falling.

~~*~~

A hazy white crept through the slits in Sloane's eyes. She tried to open her mouth, but couldn't tell if it was there to open. Focusing on the white, she finally was able to make out the square ceiling tiles so common in office buildings. Someone had cleaned her eyes.

"She's waking, sir." A bodiless voice drifted through Sloane's head.

"Our pretty little girl is waking, eh?" A familiar voice answered. Sloane was relatively certain that if she could feel right now, racks of fear would be ripping through her spine. But she felt nothing. Then the voice was at her ear.

"Sloane, my dear." The voice was soft but there was nothing gentle in it to ease her deadened fears. "It's so nice to have you. It's been overdue. I've been watching you for years, honey. Years. Longer than you know. It just wasn't right for your mother to have to deal with it, you know. Just wasn't right." The last was said so softly that Sloane realized with a jolt that despite being a complete psycho, he loved her mother. The thought made her whimper.

Her stepfather's voice became firm. "Talking to animals, thinking you can read people's thoughts and emotions. It's just not natural."

Sloane shuttered involuntarily. The voice chuckled before continuing, "Yes, I know all about it. Why do you think I made sure she was numb to it? Why do you think I made sure your curse was dampened? You *are* as crazy as a loon, Sloane. And now, you belong here, where we can take good care of you."

Silence filled the room. Sloane fought to stay awake, to beat it, but the drugs won. She was falling again with no idea how to get out. Then she didn't care.

Chapter 49

Noah was back in the cell on Monday. Verity sighed when she saw that he was covered in blood again. She quickly took care of the others, even telling another story to the boy while wiping him down and changing his sheets. The weird gilled man was missing, but Henry was back. He was sleeping soundly so she quietly left his food tray before heading back to Noah's cell.

His wings were still being forced out by the strange metal object in his back and the skin around the contraption had turned a grayish red color, swollen and infected. He had dried blood smeared down part of his face and near his lip but there were no cuts that she could see. He was breathing heavily. Verity's brows crinkled with concern. Noah was the only one who had ever been left in his cell without being cared for first and fear for him sent shivers through her core. Things here were so *wrong*.

Verity wet a cloth and started cleaning him up again. When she started to dab peroxide on his back, he moaned in pain. Verity was desperate to somehow curb the skin from infection.

"Please stop," he whispered. Verity froze with

the cloth in her hand. His hand snaked out toward her arm and then sunk back to the bedside before touching her. Verity tossed the cloth into the sink and went to her knees so she could see his face. She brushed his hair out of his eyes and ran her fingers over his cheekbone.

"What are they doing to you?" she whispered.

"They're trying to figure me out," he whispered back. He opened his yellow eyes half way and Verity could see the effort in them.

"I don't know how to help you," Verity whispered again, a tear sliding down her cheek. Noah managed a weak smile.

"I do." He reached out, grimacing in pain, and wiped the tear from her face.

"How?"

Noah's eyes slid closed as he softly whispered in her ear.

~~*~~

Liam stood staring at the map, willing it to tell him where Noah was. He could hear Brick's deep murmur as he spoke on the phone through a closed door and the coffee pot's drip echoed loudly as he tried to concentrate. He was rubbing his face when Ryan and Kam came through the front door.

"Finally got the research done on Sloane's family," Ryan said as he tossed a folder on the table. Brick came in, shoving a phone in his pocket. His annoyance slung through the air.

"Give us the condensed version," he ordered.

"We finally have a lead," Kam said, although he wasn't smiling.

"Her stepfather runs a psychiatric institute. Apparently, he's a big name in the industry." Kam met everyone's eyes before continuing, "He's also an ex-Navy Seal, top secret specialty; *interrogation*."

Andy walked out of the kitchen, a sandwich halfway to his mouth and stopped when he saw them all. The silence was heavy as everyone looked at each other, mouths grim and muscles tense.

Liam's phone rang, bringing everyone's eyes to him. He answered.

"Liam?" a soft feminine voice suddenly received all his attention.

"Yes?"

"Noah needs your help."

Chapter 50

Verity sat in her car outside of Cafe Bliss. She was afraid to go in, afraid of trusting anyone with her secret. Noah promised Liam was a friend. Noah told her that three others of his kind, what kind he didn't specify, had gone missing and that based on what he'd been experiencing, he didn't have much time. Verity shivered. Noah wouldn't tell her what they had done to him so far, but she could see that he was weaker each time she saw him.

A motorcycle pulled up two cars down and the tall rider, face hidden beneath a black helmet, jumped off as soon as it was parked and started toward the Cafe Bliss door. As he reached the door he pulled the helmet off. Red hair glinted in the sun and Verity stifled a surprised intake of breath. Noah hadn't been kidding about that. Liam somehow heard her and quickly turned from the door to look at her. Goosebumps flooded her skin as he headed to her car. She lowered the passenger window and he bent over to lean on the door.

"Noah's friend?" he asked in a deep voice. She nodded as she took in his white skin, chiseled cheekbones and bright blue eyes.

"We need to go somewhere else. There's a possibility of someone we don't trust showing up unannounced. Do you know the Mexican place on Cleveland Street?"

"Yes," Verity said nodding.

"Good. See you there," Liam said. He tapped the car door twice and headed back to his bike. Verity pulled out of the parking lot and headed toward the new meeting place.

Liam beat her there. When she pulled in he was leaning against the sleek, black bike, his helmet already off and hanging from some unseen hook on the bike. His arms were across his chest as he waited patiently for her to park and meet up with him.

"Almost thought you weren't going to show," he said as she walked up to him. He flashed a quick smile at her before his face faded into seriousness. "I'm glad you did."

"He seems to think you can help." She looked him over as they walked to the restaurant. "If you can, you'll be helping...many. He's not the only one." Liam stopped with his hand on the door and met her eyes.

"There's more? Like him?"

"Not like him, but there's..." Verity tried to find the right words. She didn't know what any of them *were,* just that they needed help.

"Others?" Liam asked. Verity nodded, and his face went solemn. They got a booth at the very back of the restaurant in a corner away from the few other late lunchers. Liam ordered a nachos appetizer for them to share and a coke. Verity ordered iced tea. When the waitress had gone, Liam gave Verity his full attention.

"I didn't get your name."

"Verity."

"Truth." Liam stated. Verity nodded, that's what her name meant. "I guess we're lucky that Noah found Truth. Which brings me to the topic of our meeting. Where is he?"

"I started working at this mental health facility a couple of months ago. I'm a nurse," Verity started saying. Liam nodded so she continued. "At first I was on the regular floors. Although I did what was asked, I started to realize that the things they do with these patients is wrong. It doesn't help them. It just turns them into vegetables. Before I had decided what to do, the owner took an interest in me. He brought me to one of the floor levels below the building and attempted drug hypnosis on me. They wanted..."

"Attempted?" Liam interrupted.

"It didn't work. They wanted me to work in another area of the building. A secret area. I was scared to death. For some reason drugs don't affect me much and now I know hypnosis doesn't either. They were over-confident, and I pretended."

"Geez," Liam said running his hand through his unruly hair.

"I know. Every day for the first week I was trying to figure out how to get out of it. Two floors down from the regular practice, they have cells with...with things in them. All different. I don't know what they do to them but these, people, are sad and scared. They're victims, no matter what they look like. My job is to bring them food, change their sheets, that type of stuff." A stray tear escaped and she wiped it away, smudging black across her cheek. Liam just watched and listened.

"One of them is just a child." She fought, but the tears ran. Liam gave her a handful of napkins and waited. After blotting them she continued. "Only one of them would talk to me, the only one who I can't figure out why he's even there. The rest barely move or say a thing. The child. He would try to hide under the sink." As Liam nodded the waitress showed up with their order. She looked at them both, set down the food and left quietly.

"Then this last week, Noah showed up in one of the cells. The rest of them came a little bit alive. It's almost like they knew him or what he was and felt hope. The second time I saw Noah, after he'd gone missing for a few days, he told me about you. I called you as soon as I got off work."

Liam rubbed his hands together as he thought and swallowed a nacho. Verity took a long drink of her tea and sighed.

"Can you draw me this place?"

"Sure." Verity flipped her place mat over and took a pen from her purse. Liam watched as the building, the lower floors, the elevator and the parking lot came into being on the paper. She asterisked the floor where they were held.

"It's in Clearwater," she said, "just before

Largo, mixed in with a bunch of other medical buildings." Liam studied the map. He leaned his head on his hand, his elbow on the table apparently deep in thought. Verity sat nervously eating the nachos.

"Security?" Liam asked.

"Yes and no," Verity answered. "In the main building, there are cameras all over the place. Once you hit the lower floors, there's nothing. I've only been on the first three lower levels. I know there's a fourth because it's on the elevator. When they disappear, I think that's where they get taken."

"Okay. Well, that's good for us. I need to get some help," he said as he pulled out his phone. He tossed nachos into his mouth periodically as he tapped the phone for a time. When he was done he looked at Verity. Concern washed over his face.

"Tell me about the others."

After Verity described everyone, Liam looked angry. He didn't even try to hide it.

"We have to do this tonight. We can't wait and let them do any more damage," Liam stated.

"I need to go with you."

"I guarantee we can take care of it. It may not be pretty but I will get those people out of there. I don't want..." he paused, obviously trying to think of a good way to tell her he didn't want her hurt or killed. Verity knew exactly what he was trying to say.

"I know. I know what you want, but I'm going. That little boy will never go with you unless I tell him it's okay." Verity's tears and fear evaporated when she thought of the little one being left behind.

"Verity, you've led us to the monster's cave. I don't think it would be..."

"Stop. Right. Now. I may seem like a silly little thing to you, but I want those people out of there and I want Doctor J to pay."

"Doctor J," Liam said softly to himself.

"That man is evil. He's the one doing all this." Verity put her glass down on the table with a little too much effort. The glass-meets-wood bang caused the nearest couple to glance over before they continued their own conversation.

Liam stared at her for an uncomfortable moment before dropping his shoulders.

"Fine," he said. "But you do what I say so I can keep you safe."

"Okay," Verity said shrugging. Liam frowned and shook his head. He looked troubled.

Verity leaned across the table, motioning him to her. He leaned over until they were just inches apart.

Verity whispered, "Do you have wings too?"

Liam nodded once and Verity pulled back to her seat and watched him silently. He pulled a wad of cash out of his pocket and placed some on the table. Then he tore off a corner of the tablecloth, wrote an address on it and handed it to her.

"This is where we're meeting in case you lose me on the way."

Verity glanced at the paper and nodded. It

was just down the street as far as she could tell.

"Now let's go meet up with the crew amassing at my place and plan our evening."

Chapter 51

Verity followed Liam who, thankfully, kept the speed down so she wouldn't lose him. A good friend back in school had died in a car accident and her heart squeezed a bit thinking of it. Since then she had become a bit of a wussy driver.

They arrived at a building downtown that looked to be eight stories high or so and had its own covered parking garage. Verity followed Liam up to the third story level. He parked in a spot marked 803 and she took the guest spot next to him. He was off his bike and striding toward the elevator before Verity had her door shut. She hurried over to him and redeemed her slowness by at least beating the elevators arrival.

They rode up in silence. Verity was glad she was wearing black jeans, a light blue button-up and flat black boots. At least she wouldn't have to worry about being in a dress or something trivial like that. Her heart hammered in her chest as she thought of Noah. Liam cocked his head at her.

"Just do as I say and you'll be fine," he said. Verity gave him a crooked smile.

"I wasn't worried about me."

Understanding flashed across Liam's face and

his eyebrows went up. Verity felt her cheeks heat up.

The elevator door opened to a long hallway. Liam led her to door 803 and swung it open. They walked through an empty hallway to the living room where a large table covered with paper and pictures sat. One wall was covered with a map of the area, full of pushpins and red lines drawn in various places, with the occasional picture. Two couches arranged in a V shape faced the map, but to Verity the people were much more interesting, especially the one standing at the point of the V.

He was massive, like an ebony tree trunk, and reminded Verity of a typical movie thug. He nodded at her, his eyes bright with intelligence. *Scratch the typical* she thought. Two scary big guys sat on the left couch, one with a nasty scar running down his face. On the right was a bronze-skinned younger boy who sat at the edge of the couch a bit away from the rest. He looked nervous. A woman sat at the other end, lounging like a cat. She smiled thinly at Verity and waved a hand to the seat between her and the boy.

Verity wondered if any of them were human. She had seen enough now to know better than trust her eyes. Sitting carefully between the boy and the woman, Verity gave her attention to Liam who was standing before them.

He chose to give introductions first which Verity appreciated. The boy was Andy, the girl Danni, the massive guy was appropriately Brick and the two on the couch were Ryan and Kam,

Kam being the one with the scar, though he smiled pleasantly enough. Then Liam held up Verity's drawing.

"We have the location and we have the basic layout," he said, "now we just have to plan how to get them all out."

"Liam?" Ryan asked, "Why is she here?" He thumbed in Verity's direction.

"There's a little boy that she believes won't leave if she's not there to get him. If we do this right, she should be fine. She's seen enough strange things in the last couple of weeks that we are the least of her worries."

Ryan nodded with satisfaction. Then Kam piped up, "What about him?" He glanced at Andy, who looked like he wanted to disappear.

"He has a skill that is perfect for what we're going to be doing tonight." Liam said. Kam didn't look excited but didn't say anything more. Liam smiled though it didn't reach his eyes. "He's a Displacer. Need I say more?" Kam raised his eyebrows and looked at Andy a bit differently. Verity wondered what the heck that was.

"Here's what I think we should do," Liam said as he turned his back to them and spread the place mat on the table. This must have been a signal as they all surrounded the table, Verity too.

Liam spoke quickly and concisely, drawing lines and symbols that were foreign to Verity. No one objected, though Brick's deep, rustic voice occasionally injected support or suggestions which helped to formulate the plan. At one point, when Verity had stopped paying attention, they all looked at Andy with approval and smiles. Verity didn't understand it, but she knew what she needed to do. That was all she really cared about, that and one other thing, a good-looking blond, but she kept that to herself. She was fairly confident that this crew of *people* could handle that part just fine.

Brick went around the table questioning each person on their role. Like a drill sergeant he made them repeat their instructions until it was exactly what he wanted to hear. Verity caught the smell of coffee wafting through the room and thought having some might be a good idea. She wanted as much extra power as she could get.

When Brick looked at her she stated, "I'm to stick with Andy. We'll go to the boy so I can retrieve him and get him out safely. I follow Andy and do whatever he says." Brick nodded. Verity's eyes flickered to the kitchen.

"Go grab yourself a cup while we wrap up."

Verity didn't need to be told twice. As she headed toward the kitchen she heard Liam ask Danni if she had everything she needed. She found sugar and cream set out and several empty mugs. After quickly preparing a cup she took a gulp and almost spilled her coffee down her shirt when Danni's voice came from right behind her.

"It's funny, most of them drink it but not a one of them actually needs it. At least not like you and I do." Danni proceeded to pour herself a cup. Holding it up she said, "My second this evening. I'm just glad I had a huge meal. I'm going to need some serious energy tonight."

Verity nodded and smiled, not sure what to say. Food was definitely not at the forefront of her mind.

"Don't worry, honey, we've all had a first day. Yours'll be over soon." She left Verity standing in the kitchen wondering what that meant.

Chapter 52

They wouldn't let Verity bring her own car. She ended up in a matte black van sitting next to Andy. Kam was driving and Ryan sat in the passenger seat. Liam had gone with Danni and Brick in another nondescript van. From Kam and Ryan's conversation Verity was able to understand that they had already scouted the outside of the building and knew where the cameras were. Liam and Brick were going to take care of those first.

There would be nurses and at least one doctor on night shift but none of them should be on the lower levels. At least Verity didn't think so. She watched as the other van turned down a side street near their destination. Her van continued another block.

Streaks of what felt like fire flies started running through her veins. Andy turned to her, his face puzzled. She gave a weak smile which he returned in earnest.

"This stuff's all new to me too," he whispered. Verity smiled wider glad to know she was in similar company.

"You have a key part in all of this," she whispered back. She wasn't really worried about being overheard. Ryan and Kam were rambling up front, laughing and making fun of each other like this was stuff they did every day. For all Verity knew, they did.

Andy shrugged, "Apparently my ability is rare."

Verity nodded, impressed. "I guess I'm going to have a very interesting night then."

Andy leaned toward her, his face solemn, "I think that's an understatement."

"We're here folks!" Ryan practically hollered at them. He turned around in his seat with a huge grin on his face. "Let's go have some fun."

Verity cringed a little.

~~*~~

A neighborhood bordered a small section of medical facilities. Liam parked the van in the shadows of a tree next to a dark and silent house. Everyone got out walked to the fence at the rear of their destination. Brick smiled and gave Liam a thumbs-up before morphing into a particularly large swirl of shadows. The swirl moved easily over the fence and across the parking lot to the back left of the building. As the shadows twisted, they lengthened up twelve feet and a bodiless claw pushed out of the whirling mass to take out the first camera. Moving to the other corner the claw took out a second camera. The shadows moved to the back door and held there like a black hole.

As Verity had said, a single guard opened the

door to check on the cameras. The door slammed shut behind him and before he could react, a mini-tornado had trapped him in a rage of swirling madness. The guard crumbled to the ground. Brick solidified and his white teeth reflected in the streetlight as he smiled. Liam withheld a chuckle. Suffocating them until they passed out wasn't Liam's preference but today he would go with the flow. At least the guy wouldn't have anything interesting to report later. He'd probably be sent in for a physical.

Liam and Danni moved toward the building while Brick went back to the fence to wait for the others. As planned, Brick had placed a card to stop the locking mechanism and Liam slowly opened the back door. His skin was roiling as he peeked inside. The silence was like a tomb. Apparently, they hadn't set off any alarms.

Stepping inside they found themselves in a short hallway. The smell of burnt coffee from an open door down the hall told Liam there was a break room.

Danni felt the walls in a few different places, then knelt to touch the floor. She looked at Liam and nodded affirmation. He pursed his lips and held up a finger, telling her to wait. A noise caught his attention but he quickly discarded it when he realized it was a snore coming from the next room up the hall.

There were no shadows for Liam to use to his advantage so he simply walked by the break room entry hoping it was vacant.

It was. He looked back at Danni and she

followed him down the hallway. At the end he turned left and strode with purpose, passing an office where a chubby nurse sat at a desk snoring her shift away. He neared the door that he was looking for just as a security officer rounded the corner ahead. The man ran toward Liam as he pulled out his gun. Liam met him in the hall, easily side swiped the gun and grabbed the carotid artery in the man's neck. He passed out instantly and Liam caught him and lowered him gently to the ground. Taking his keys, Liam found the storage room Verity had described and unlocked the door

As he was about to enter he felt an odd twist in his chest, a subtle pull that made him pause. Despair ran through him ever so briefly and then was gone. He ignored the anomaly and he walked into the room where he found the elevator.

Danni glanced at the prone man before following Liam into the room. She once more felt the walls and floor. She grimaced at him and pulled her pack from her waist taking out all manner of items. Liam left her to it and moved the man into the breakroom. He went back and leaned against the door watching the hallway with an occasional glance at Danni's preparations. The strange anxious feeling from earlier didn't return. After a few moments he smelled something wrong and glanced over. Danni had built a small pebble circle, put what looked like weeds and hair in the middle and had lit it on fire. There didn't seem to be smoke, just a strange smell.

When she started to whisper over the fire it changed from orange and blue to gold and red. Danni threw something else in it, whispered a word and the fire died. Danni felt the floor then stood up and sauntered over to Liam.

"One protection spell, broken. You know I am good for more things than this right?" She smiled up at him. There was a time when he would have responded in kind, but no longer.

"Hmph. Let's signal the others," he answered and headed back down the hall. He heard her shuffled steps several feet behind him.

At the back door, he leaned out an arm and waved. Four dark shadows crossed the lot followed by Verity. They slipped through the door, bringing the security guard with them. Brick laid the man on the floor of the break room next to the man Liam had knocked out, and unplugged the phone from the wall. He brought it out with him, closing the door behind and bending the handle. Liam smiled with approval. Brick duplicated his efforts at the sleeping nurse's office and they headed to the storage room in silence. When they were packed into the elevator, Verity hit the button to Level C. Her heart fluttered in anticipation. Liam patted her on the shoulder.

The elevator didn't move. Liam looked at Andy.

"You're ready?" he asked. Eyes wide, Andy nodded and he and Liam stepped out of the elevator.

"You know what to do," he encouraged as Andy placed both hands around one of his forearms. Andy started to shift. It spread over him quickly and moved to engulf Liam. Liam raised his free hand and waved before they vanished into swirls of darkness. Verity stared as they melted through the floor.

Chapter 53

Sweat broke out over Verity's skin, her heart pumped like a sledgehammer. Moments ticked by, Verity's breathing too loud in her head. Brick stood outside the elevator while she and the others stood inside quietly waiting.

Finally, a mechanical pop brought everyone to attention. The elevator doors snicked shut. Verity pressed the button to Level C and was promptly shoved to the back of the elevator. Kam stood just to the front and left of her as the elevator smoothly descended into the depths of the institute.

Danni lounged, her shoulder resting against the side wall, her hip pushed out, elbow resting suggestively. She turned and caught Verity looking at her. She smiled and raised her eyes up and down. Verity's eyes widened as Danni pulled a gun that was tucked in the back of her shorts. Danni snickered.

Ryan stood front, center until the elevator came to a stop. He waved everyone down and followed his own advice going down to one knee. The elevator suddenly became very crowded. Just before the door shooshed open, both Kam and Ryan's skin started to whirl.

Verity felt her chest tighten. Fear crawled through her skin.

"It's clear," Liam's voice came from the hall, "Verity?"

Ryan and Kam's skin stopped whirling as fast as it had started and they parted to allow Verity through. She felt self-conscious with their impassive eyes on her as she passed between them.

"Where's Andy?" Verity asked just as Brick literally came through the back wall, Andy in toe, arms hanging on to Brick for what looked like dear life. Andy's eyes were wide. Brick was smiling.

"Damn, that's a rush." Brick's eyes were shining. Liam just looked at him.

"He's not here," he said.

"No," Verity whispered. She looked up at Liam. "He must be downstairs. I hope." The last was said quietly.

Liam turned to the others. "Let's get everyone out of here, then we'll find Noah." He motioned Brick and Verity toward the cells. Kam, Danni and Ryan took up the rear.

Verity ran up to scale boy's cell, keys jangling from her hands. A glance told her what she needed to know and she turned to Liam shaking her head. She ran past the next two cells, giving them barely a glance as they had always been empty. The next one was the boy. He sat on the bed. His fine pale hair had been slicked down with water and he smiled when he saw her. She unlocked the door and he jumped off the bed and straight into her arms.

"I knew you would come," he said. He saw Liam, Kam and Ryan and positively beamed at them. They gave each other a knowing look and smiled back at the boy. Verity didn't understand the look but was pleased that he held on to her tightly. He turned to her, smiled and gave her back a pat.

"You can put me down, there are others." He slid down her and landed happily on his feet.

"Stay close, little one," Verity warned him as she quickly ran to the next cell. She stared down at the lady in the water. Her eyes were slightly milky, her gills barely fluttering.

Verity sorted through the keys. As she unlocked the door she turned to Liam and said, "I don't know what to do for her but if she doesn't get help very soon, I don't think she'll make it."

The door swung open and Verity moved out of the way.

"Shit," Kam said. Verity scrutinized his face. He was frowning. "How did they get a Siren?"

Liam knelt and gazed down at her. She didn't move and he looked up at Ryan. "Think you can handle her?"

Ryan paused for a half second before pulling his shirt off and stuffing it into a black bag slung over his shoulder. Verity realized that Kam and Liam had black bags as well. Ryan moved past her and leaned over the pool. His skin started to roil and turned a dull gray color. Verity watched as his skin hardened. He looked exactly the same as always except with slick-looking, gray skin.

She wanted to touch it to see what it felt like.

Moving very slowly, Ryan put a large hand over the back of the Siren's neck. The moment he gripped her, she flung her feet toward him but he was ready for it. Her feet hit him but bounced off like rubber. He raised her by the neck to meet his eyes. Her milky round eyes stared at him but that wasn't what scared Verity. The slit of a mouth opened exposing sharp, jagged teeth as she stretched her mouth wider than it should go. Ryan shoved his other hand under her jaw and pushed her mouth closed. He pulled her close to him.

"I don't know how much you understand, girl, but I am trying to help you. I'll bring you to the ocean."

Her eyes widened even further, if that was possible and she went limp in his arms. He pulled her out of the pool and turned to Andy.

"We've got to hurry." He and Andy rushed toward the wall where Brick came through earlier. As they ran, wings sprouted from his back. Just before hitting the wall, Ryan slung the Siren over one arm and grabbed Andy's shoulder. They vanished through the wall.

Verity wasted no more time and ran to Henry's cell. He was waiting for her and smiled when he saw her.

"Ah, my dear. You couldn't leave us behind then?"

"Of course not, Henry." She unlocked his door and he gave a formal bow to them all.

"I regret that your friend has not returned. I

can only imagine he would be in the surgery or in solitary."

"How familiar are you with that floor?" Liam asked.

"Unfortunately, I've visited both so I can help you there."

"Good," Liam said. He looked back at Kam. "Get the boy and Verity out of here. We'll go get Noah."

Kam nodded. He beckoned Verity and she took the boys hand. They followed him to the back wall just as Andy came through it. He was looking a little pale. Verity left the boy with them and went to a cabinet in the corner. She pulled out a bottle of water and handed it to Andy. He nodded thanks and drank the whole thing. After a deep breath, he turned to the young boy.

"Hi," He said smiling. The boy smiled back.

"I'm ready, Verity." The boy turned to look at her and held out a hand. Verity took it and gave a light squeeze, his hand cool and soft.

"We're going to have to get cozy," Andy said. "Kam has to carry us all the way up. Hang on tight to the boy, I'll hold onto you and Kam will hold on to me. Don't let go. Ever."

Chapter 54

Verity nodded at Andy through a neck stiff with alarm. She glanced at Kam before picking up the boy and hugging him close. Andy hesitated only slightly before wrapping his arms around her waist. Kam wrapped his arms around them all. Andy's skin whirled and turned, enveloping them all in a foggy cloud. Verity heard Kam's shirt rip. She couldn't see but she thought it must be his wings.

Walking together to the wall, Verity shut her eyes when they reached it and went straight through. The air was dense and it was hard to breath. The strange sounds of concrete rubbing together, tearing and paper crinkling filled her ears. She was too scared to open her eyes and just held the boy close. She consciously felt Andy's arms around her and tried to breathe slowly.

Suddenly there was fresh air. Verity opened her eyes to open sky and then fell to her knees clutching the boy so tight he squeaked. She loosened her arms and gulped in air. Verity did not share Brick's idea of a rush. The boy pulled away and started whispering. Listening more carefully she heard him hissing and slurring, the sounds catching on the wind and rolling around them. Verity noticed that they had come up on the other side of the fence surrounding the institute and were sitting in a small patch of dark trees, bushes and grass. She glanced back at Kam who was sitting on the ground, his wings gone and shirt hanging in shreds. She saw his teeth in the darkness, a smile, and knew he was okay.

Then she saw Andy. He was lying on his side, knees drawn up to his chest with his eyes closed. She crawled over to him and put a hand on his forehead. His eyes flickered open and he gave a small smile before he whispered.

"I've never done it that much with so many people. I'll be okay."

Verity sighed with relief and he closed his eyes again. She stood and walked over to Kam. "Can you walk?"

He huffed at her. She took that as a yes. She went to the boy and took his hand. Without turning back to Kam she said, "Let's get to the van. We'll be safer there."

"Not yet," the boy said as he smiled up at her, "she's coming."

"Who's coming, little one?"

"Momma."

Verity jumped as Kam was suddenly beside her. "Let go of his hand and back away." Verity didn't let go but she turned to face him.

"Why on earth would I do that?"

Kam grabbed her free hand and started gently pulling her toward him before stopping abruptly. The boy's hand slipped away from her.

"That's why," he whispered. "Don't look her in the face."

A chill went down Verity's spine as she slowly turned her head. A white gown flowed in the breezeless night. She had to look up and up some more just to see the arms and neck. Iridescent skin, the same as the boy's, sparkled in the thin moonlight. Long silvery-white hair flowed down to a small waist. Verity so wanted to look at the woman's face but Kam had successfully frightened her, so she stood, heart quickening and body still.

The soft whispering hisses of the boy filled the air, dancing on her skin. Out of the corner of her eye she saw him hold his mother's legs, or what she thought must be legs beneath the flowing dress. A slim hand patted the boy's head and the body floated so close that Verity could smell wild flowers and freshly cut grass. A voice, scratchy and husky as though unused to making the sounds, wrapped around Verity like a mother's hug.

"I am grateful to you, all of you, for bringing me back my son. I am used to receiving, not giving, but I shall grant you one kindness for doing what I could not. My son shall remember you and I will know when my favor is due."

Her hand came up and warm fingers brushed Verity's cheek. The wild flower smell engulfed her, delivering a peaceful lull until she felt something clamp on her wrist and then a stabbing pain shot up her arm. Verity pulled her hand away and looked down. The little boy was licking blood from his lips. She looked at her wrist and the small bite marks, blood started to seep down onto her hand.

"I shall remember you, Verity," he said happily. The two turned away from her, hand in hand, and vanished into the bushes like ghosts. Verity sat down abruptly on the dewy grass and stared at her bloody hand. Kam appeared beside her and looked at it briefly then laid her hand in her lap. She looked at him, but she didn't really see him. She did hear him though.

"Crash course in the Fae."

Chapter 55

Liam watched Verity and the others go through the wall before entering the elevator with Brick, Danni and Henry in tow, Verity's keys tucked safely in his pocket. Danni still had her gun out and Brick leaned against the wall of the elevator, face blank. Henry stood quietly, hands clasped in front of him.

Everyone except Henry was moving instinctively. Liam and Brick stood at the front, their skin roiling, Liam's more obvious, the gray swirls caressing him into shadow. Brick's already dark skin writhed like serpents. Danni stood behind them, gun held low, the safety off as she focused on the door. Henry stood in the rear, seemingly relaxed, tension just touching his gaunt features.

As the doors started to slide apart, Danni moved to the right slightly. If guns were blazing, bullets wouldn't harm the Guardians and she knew it.

A quiet electrical hum was all that met them. Liam and Brick moved into the small hallway. There were two doors to their right and one in front. Brick glanced at Henry. He was slowly coming out the elevator, eyes a bit wider. He pointed to the door in front and kept shuffling his way into the hallway.

Brick tried the door. When it didn't open easily, he pulled the knob off and shoved the door open. A tall, greasy man with yellow teeth stood up in surprise. Brick bolted forward and cold-cocked him in the jaw before he could say a word. The man slumped to the ground. People didn't get hit by Brick and have anything to say, at least for a while. Brick turned and gave a satisfied smile to Liam and Danni hovering outside.

Everyone moved forward to the next door. This one wasn't locked. Brick entered and stopped suddenly. Liam almost ran in to him. Sidestepping he was able to see into the room. About the size of a dentist's office it had a chair in the center, a chair that held someone. Liam crossed the few feet and looked the man over. He was young, scaled and dead. Liam looked back at Brick and shook his head.

Leaving the room, they returned to Henry who was holding the elevator doors open.

"Was he there?" he whispered. Liam shook his head no. It didn't seem necessary to give any more information. Henry pointed to the two doors on the side. He looked at Liam and then Brick, ignoring Danni.

"Solitary," he said quietly.

Brick went to the first door and forced it open with a shove from his shoulder and a twist on the handle.

Something tugged at Liam's senses, a pull

made him rush toward the door. Brick stood sideways, giving Liam just enough room to slip in. Inside was hot, dark and wet. A winged creature lay on the ground in the corner. Liam knelt by the contorted wings, the body curled up beneath them.

"Brick. Could use a hand here."

Brick forced himself into the small space and they lifted Noah together. A low moan echoed from the bent body. Maneuvering him out of the tiny space, Brick took him and slung him gently over his shoulder, allowing the wings to spread out behind him.

He looked at Liam. "If this is the shape he's in, I don't think we can count on any one else being alive."

Liam nodded. He didn't think so either. Just in case, he wrenched the handle of the other room and swung the door open. The smell of death permeated his senses but it was empty.

Henry waited within the elevator. Danni had joined him, standing quietly and without emotion as Brick stepped inside, twisting his body to avoid harming his burden further. There was no room left without bending Noah further. Liam waved his hand in an upward gesture.

"Go up, get him out of here. I'll call the elevator back down." Brick nodded, the others hidden behind him. The doors closed and Liam waited until he heard it ascend before hitting the button.

He leaned his back against the wall waiting. It was so quiet he could hear a flea jump. It seemed eerie to him that they'd met so little resistance. A sharp pain stabbed his chest. He looked down in shock, half expecting to find something jammed through his body, but there was nothing there. His skin still roiled with protection. The pull he had felt earlier flared ten-fold. An image came to mind.

Sloane. Flashes of angst and fear. Overwhelming helplessness overtook his senses. He slammed his fist into the wall, punching through the drywall, bending the metal studs. The elevator doors snicked open and he threw his body in and hit the top button. Pacing like a caged animal until the door opened he found himself at ground level. He had to get to the main elevators. He ran.

Chapter 56

Dreamlike, Sloane tucked inside herself and gathered energy. She searched and pulled from every pocket she could find. The poisons in her system started to ease out, pushed out by the thick and sluggish energy. A sweaty dark film began to gleam on her skin. The effort tore at her, ripping away her strength. Only pure adrenalin kept her conscious.

Panicked voices echoed around her.

Her intake of breath sounded like a bear's growl as she flung her eyes open and took in the two nurses frantically jabbering and working to inject more drugs into her system.

"No more." Sloane's voice was foreign and ragged. She looked at the two ladies, one older with heavy wrinkles and a floral nurse's top; the other too thin and pale with large brown eyes. Not with her hands, they still wouldn't work. Sloane shoved with her mind. *Get away from me!*

Something deep inside her pooled and burst forth into the room. Both women flew backward. The thin one slammed head first into the wall and slid to the floor. The other simply fell over and stopped moving.

Sloane couldn't fall back since she had never

moved, but the power did. It soaked back in, settling into her with a sleepy sigh. A door slammed open and she heard footsteps coming at an alarming speed. A familiar red head, blue eyes wide with concern came into view. She smiled and closed her eyes, finally calm.

~~*~~

Liam rushed to Sloane like a fire was chasing the oxygen in his blood only to find himself sprawled on the floor a couple of feet from her bed. He had run straight into an invisible wall.

A high-pitched laugh rang out from the far side of the room. A slow clap followed. Liam shifted as he leapt up, wings tearing from his back, his head and limbs wrenched by the speed of the transformation.

The clapping came in earnest this time.

"Impressive, Liam," she said from the shadows of the room. His black eyes watched her warily and he didn't answer.

"You can't have her, Guardian. She's worm bait no matter which way you look at it. When she's gone, your bond will be broken and you will belong to me. Since your kind only bonds once, that is a letdown, but we'll make the best of it."

Liam growled. "What are you going on about, Danni?" he asked through clenched teeth. "Why don't you get it through your paper-thin mind? You can't have me."

Danni's form flickered in annoyance. Then

she stood several feet in front of him, in Sloane's form.

"If it's just the look you want, I can do that for you. I would do quite a few things to gain your attentions." She drew her hands down her body. "I'm quite talented, you know."

Liam shook his head in disgust. "Why me, Danni?"

She shrugged. "Why not? I need a challenge every so often. You must understand, otherwise you wouldn't have stayed on as an active Guardian for so long after your time was up."

"You can't have me." He growled, "I'm taken."

Danni chuckled. "Not for long, my love. Not for long. The old fool thinks he can cure her but all he does is kill. And she *will* be killed. Her skin's not tough like yours. She'll die."

Danni shimmered and her normal blond-haired form appeared. Liam almost shook with the effort of containing his anger.

"Not so fast," a strong female voice said from the entrance of the room. Liam turned to see a blindingly beautiful blond in a soft flowing blue dress striding slowly and purposefully toward them. She glanced at Liam and smiled.

"I've always wanted to say that," she said. Liam cocked his head and backed up enough to keep both women in view.

"You bitch," the lady in blue said to Danni. "You think you can take whatever you want, don't you? Just take, take, take and never suffer the consequences?"

The lady stopped just a few feet from Liam,

her eyes steady on Danni. He didn't know what the hell was going on but he knew a cat fight when he saw one. He crouched down to watch.

Danni laughed. "Still full of purity and light, I see." She stopped laughing and glared. "But you're nothing. Ex-communicated and drained of any power. You're less than nothing. I don't even know why they allow you to live."

The lady smiled. She stood still, hands clasped together casually in front while her dress rippled in a nonexistent breeze.

"Your mind is as broken as your heart, my old friend. You still only see what you wish." The lady's face turned sad. "For that I am sorry."

She waved a hand toward Sloane and brought up the other, palm out toward Danni.

"Take her and leave, Guardian."

Liam didn't wait for a second request. He went through the now vanquished wall and scooped Sloane from the bed.

Danni's high-pitched shrieks filled the room but whatever forcefield the lady in blue had thrown up held her steadfast.

Liam kicked out the single window, bent back the bars and took to the sky with Sloane cradled possessively in his arms.

Chapter 57

Dr. J stood fuming in the room where Sloane had been. This had not been the way his plan was meant to play out. He had misunderstood the strength of Danni's power, or lack thereof. The demon had obviously escaped with Sloane through the window. A three-foot wide burn mark on the floor indicated what he assumed was Danni's demise.

He looked around and played out what must have happened. He had underestimated and would need to research and do more tests before he could rid the world of these demons. Using their blood and DNA to improve his race was futile. His experiments had failed, one after the other, but he knew how to kill them. They just needed to be gone. *Abominations, all of them*, he thought.

Sighing, he thought of Clara and what he would tell her.

Hal, the useless man had been knocked unconscious downstairs, cleared his throat behind him. Dr. J. turned and glared.

"Put the nurses downstairs in holding. We'll interrogate and remove their memories. The security guard should be brought up here. Then call the cops. Let's get them looking for our missing patient too. The more help the merrier."

~~*~~

He stood in the lobby of his institute with new purpose. The police were combing the upper floors and finding everything in place save the broken window and burn mark. Of course, the security guard remembered nothing. The detectives were stumped, that he knew, but they would look for her. Dr. J also knew that he would need to find a new place to carry out his work. He would find the answers he was looking for. Of that he was certain.

Chapter 58

Liam watched Sloane as she lay unconsciousness in his bed. He had flown directly to the den. The others had beaten him there. Noah was resting in his room hooked up to a machine for re-hydration while they scrambled to get a qualified doctor. Verity had left his side only to make sure Sloane would be okay and to care for her own odd bite mark, and that only at Kam's insistence.

Liam brushed a strand of hair from Sloane's face and allowed himself to trace the line of her eyebrow down her cheekbone. He found himself looking at her full lips. Her scent overwhelmed his sanity. He wasn't sure if he would have the opportunity again, wasn't sure how she felt about anything. He leaned in and placed his lips on hers, breathed in her scent and imagined those lips responding.

Before he completely lost it, he moved away from the bed and walked out the door.

Sloane's eyelids fluttered open. After several blinks, she could make out a door in the dark room. Bringing a hand to her lips, the vaguest sensation came to mind. She smiled and drifted off into a most peaceful sleep.

~~*~~

When she woke a warm hand was gently holding hers. She smiled, turning in anticipation and was instead surprised.

"Nia?" she croaked. Nia smiled and squeezed her hand before holding a cup of water with a straw to her. Sloane took a couple of long pulls before settling back to her pillow. She raised her eyebrows and crossed her arms over her chest.

"It's a long story. Can I tell it later and you just be happy that I'm here?"

Sloane watched her for a long moment before nodding and reaching out to her friend. Nia jumped up and hugged her. When they finally pulled away Sloane felt a sudden sense of dread, an emptiness in her heart.

"Where's Liam?" she whispered. Nia held up a finger and went to the door, she peered out. After a moment, a very old, stooped woman with gray hair and wearing a bright, floral dress entered the room. When their eyes met, Sloane knew there was nothing that would get past the sharp mind residing there. The woman made Sloane a little bit scared.

Nia's hand touched her shoulder. "This is Aggie. She's an Aspie and she'll be working with you, Sloane."

Sloane's mouth dropped. "But how do you...?"

"Not now, my dear friend," Nia said with a sorrowful smile. "I have to leave now. They let me stay until you woke."

"But..."

"I will see you soon for a long talk and a good movie." With that Nia blew her a kiss and glided from the room.

Aggie sat down and looked at Sloane. Sloane looked everywhere else.

"I know you're nervous, child, but I'm not going to bite," Aggie said. Her voice was low and gravelly, like she'd smoked several packs a day for years.

Sloane finally looked at her and Aggie cracked a crooked, denture-filled smile. That brought a small curve to Sloane's lips. A thought ran across her mind and Aggie answered before she could voice it.

"Yes, Aspie's can read each other." Sloane nodded, one question finally answered. Then she looked at Aggie and realized she couldn't see a hue.

"But I don't see yours. There's nothing there at all."

"It's the drugs. They dull your mind, stunt your senses. Once you've rested up a bit, we'll get you through a nice cleansing detox and I would venture to say you will read better than ever. Lord knows how long you've been given those hideous things. Then we'll get you well taught."

Eyes like saucers, Sloane nodded and thought of him again.

"He's been called away to another mission, your Liam," Aggie stated bluntly. Sloane blushed.

"I wouldn't call him mine, but he's my friend,"

Sloane said, "He saved me."

"Pah," Aggie grumbled, "He's yours alright. If nothing stops him, he'll be back."

"What could stop him?" Sloane whispered.

Aggie raised an eyebrow at her. "Why, life, of course."

Chapter 59

Beside herself with worry, Verity was flattening the carpet between the couches with her pacing. It had taken several days but someone named Keanan had finally managed to get a doctor flown in from 'headquarters'. They had been in the room with Noah for hours.

She was alone in her worries. Andy had been sent to study at the library. Aggie had dropped Sloane off for another day of the detox program and Verity had been left to wait. Keanan had tried to talk her into going home but Verity had refused. She had taken care of Noah for this long, she would see it through. Keanan finally backed down and had let her stay.

She walked around the couches for the umpteenth time when her stomach growled. Food. If nothing else, she could cook for the guys working so hard to help Noah.

An hour later, Verity found herself quite pleased with her efforts. Steak Marsala, seasoned zucchini and bread rolls were almost ready. Wondering who had thought to buy zucchini she went to sit on the couch to wait the last few minutes for everything to finish.

Just tucking her feet under her, she heard it.

Soft at first, then reaching her ears in a volume that melted the tension in her heart.

Laughter.

Verity pressed her hand to her chest and felt the final vestiges of worry melt away just as the timer went off.

Pulling out four plates, Verity divvied up the meal. She only had to wait a moment before the door to Noah's room opened and Keanan joined her in the kitchen. He was of Asian descent, muscular and trim, but tall.

"Please tell me that's for us," he said with smile and then cocked his head and nodded positively. "He's going to be fine."

Verity leaned back against the counter and closed her eyes. Whatever fear was left blew away and she couldn't help the tears that sprang up and leaked down her cheeks. She felt Keanan's warm hand on her shoulder and quickly buried her face in her hands, embarrassed.

"Seriously though," he whispered, "this is for us, right?"

Verity laughed and shook her head at him. Wiping the tears away, she grabbed two plates and headed toward the bedroom.

"Let's eat!" Keanan bellowed happily and was on her heels with the other two plates. When Verity walked in she almost dropped the plates.

Noah sat on the side of the bed dressed only in a pair of faded blue jeans. His color had returned and his sculptured chest was a sun kissed bronze. He was chatting amiably with the doctor, whose name Verity had missed or forgotten.

Standing, he smiled broadly and bowed low to Verity. She caught just a glimpse of his back. His wings were gone and only a pink blemish was left where the metal had been removed.

Verity held out a plate and he took it gratefully. He glanced at the doctor who quickly turned and caught Keanan at the door. The doctor took one of the plates from Keanan and gestured him out. When the door closed behind him, Verity gave Noah a puzzled look. He took her plate and put it on the side table next to his. She stood nervously wondering what was happening when he turned and stood glowing before her.

"Verity," he said, his voice deep and rough.

"Yes..." she answered, still puzzled even though her heart twitched.

"I am dying to give you a hug for helping me. Would that be okay with you?"

Verity froze. She wanted the hug but now that he was okay, she worried that he wouldn't need her anymore. Would the hug be closure? Would he be done with her now? Why would she expect anything different?

Noah stepped back, hands out slightly.

"Sorry, I didn't mean to freak you out," he said, his voice the soft and low tone she was accustomed to.

Verity reached out and touched one of his hands. She shook her head. "It's not that."

He looked down at her through his intense

golden cat eyes. Verity quivered under his gaze but didn't break contact. The moment seemed to go on forever before Verity came to the only conclusion that made sense. She wasn't the only one who was scared.

She smiled and raised her arms. A grin spread across his lips making her heart jump as he wrapped his arms around her, lifting her from the ground. She tucked her arms around his neck like a feather boa and took in his scent, the feel of his skin. Verity's feet dangled as he held her tight and pressed his face into her shoulders and neck.

"You're my dark angel," he whispered into her neck. "Thank you."

Verity could only pull him closer. There were no words.

Chapter 60

The detox program was one of the most miserable experiences of Sloane's life and she'd barely started. She sat in the sauna, a sweat drenched towel beneath her. Book in hand, she tried to make out the words but they blurred and danced before her eyes. Closing the book, she tossed its sogginess down on the bench.

"This sucks," she stated.

"It's them chemicals coming out, honey. It'll go away eventually."

Sloane glanced up and met Peggy's big, brown eyes. Peggy gave her a sympathetic smile and Sloane pouted back. Peggy was a friggin monster physically and that was saying something compared to Sloane. Close to seven feet in height and built like a brick shit house, not surprisingly she was a cop. She had been exposed to some nasty chemicals during a drug raid on top of being shot and drugged to hell and back. That had brought her to the center for what she called her 'cleansing'.

The third person contributing to the rank smell in the sauna was just a kid who was maybe sixteen. Armand was short and skinny with the gaunt look of a drug user. He didn't talk and just sat in the sauna in his own misery. Unlike Peggy, who had been on the program for almost a month now, Armand was new like Sloane. She knew exactly what he was going through as she stared at her feet in fascination, noticing the pretty colored trail they left when she kicked them up and down. It was kind of nice to see the vibrant color. She hadn't been able to see hues since leaving the institution.

Peggy sniffed loudly before speaking. "You say your step-dad gave you them drugs without you even knowin' about it?"

Sloane's head turned interminably slow and she felt her lips part from her teeth in what she hoped was a smile. Peggy observed her and shook her head, grumbling, "I sure hope they find that bastard."

"Me too," Sloane murmured as she lifted her hand and waved it, watching the pretty colors. Armand noticed. He lifted his hand as well and a small smile appeared. He moved his hand back and forth in rapture.

"Hey, Larson!" Peggy hollered. The sauna door opened and a short, broad-shouldered bald guy stuck his head in.

"What's up, Peggy?" he asked.

She pointed at a thumb toward Sloane and Armand. "I think they might need s'more water."

Larson nodded and smiled. He left to get the water jug, closing the door behind him.

Sloane's mind went to Liam briefly. Then she waited for the door to open again. She sighed in contentment. The door's movement made a full rainbow of pretty colors.

~~*~~

It took exactly forty-six days for Sloane to complete her detox program. She could barely remember anything from the first three weeks. Sweating in the sauna was a piece of cake after that. On day twenty-four the hues came back. Sloane had been torn between elation and the dread of being weird again, no longer able to just fit in.

Armand had woken up from his drug stupor about the same time. She got him to open up a bit by pulling out a deck of Uno cards and threatening to slay his ass. No one could resist an Uno challenge. They settled into a nice Uno routine until the day he brought out a deck of cards and taught her Texas Hold 'Em. Sloane was hooked. She was intrigued too as she watched him over time. His hue turned from a depressed blue-green to a barely-there light yellow.

His family visited occasionally. Their fear and worry was hidden from Armand but clear as day to Sloane. She had enjoyed watching his parents and sister's hues change when they realized he was going to be all right.

On day thirty-five the emotions started to roll in. Within two days, the emotions were accompanied by thoughts and visions. Sloane learned how to mask them almost as soon as they showed up. It seemed so easy to throw up a wall to block the cacophony in her mind. The silence was so much more bearable.

Peggy finished the program a week and a half after Sloane started. Everything was so vague then Sloane hoped she had given a proper farewell. Peggy was one of those old souls who really gave a shit about taking the evil out of society.

Before picking up her gym bag, Sloane threw her arms around Larson and gave him a tight hug.

"Thank you so much, Larson. This hell journey has been one of the best things that could have happened to me."

"My pleasure," he said and laughed, patting her on the back before releasing her to Aggie's open arms where another grateful hug ensued.

Feeling healthy once more, Sloane left the building vibrant and alert, with only an ache in her heart to dampen her mood.

Chapter 61

"Stop fighting it girl!"

Sloane's eyes narrowed further. "It's too much," she growled through clenched teeth.

"You've been shutting it out for so long it only *seems* like too much. It's really just normal. Now stop being stubborn and let it *all* in. I can't teach you to control it if you don't let it in."

"I didn't know it was blocked all this time. What does come in is more than I want." Sloane closed her eyes removing the view of people absolutely chock full of thoughts and pictures and emotion as they rushed through the mall. She put her head in her hands while her ass started to fall asleep on the hard bench.

"There is no too much, Sloane. There is only non-confront. Now CONFRONT IT!"

Sloane lifted her head with a loud sigh. She imagined kicking down the mental walls with the new moves Noah had taught her. Then she watched in horror as they crashed down and the voices, thoughts, and feelings came rushing in. A thunderstorm of emotion crashed in to her and she grimaced in pain.

I hope they have this shirt in red.
What the hell do I get her?

I wonder how much more I can steal.
Why doesn't he like me?
I hate the fucking mall.
I'm starved.
Where's mommy...I want mommy.

Sloane's head snapped to attention. Her eyes roved the food court in front of her like a stalking cat.

"Good. Something caught your attention. Focus on it, Sloane. Let the rest drift to the side," Aggie directed.

"I've done this before," Sloane mumbled as she lurched from the bench and turned around. She started one way only to feel the emotion fade. Turning about, she headed toward the JC Penney, following the fear and the tearful cries echoing in her mind.

A woman dressed casually bolted from a store, nearly missing Sloane as she searched frantically, tears running down her face.

"Brian!" the woman yelled into the bustling crowd. Sloane focused on the small boy.

"Brian?" she wondered.

"Huh?" she heard and stopped, glancing back at Aggie who gave her an encouraging smile.

"Brian," Sloane focused her thought, "your mom is trying to find you. You need to step out where she can see you."

"Oh," echoed in Sloane's head. Scanning, she watched as a small boy stepped from behind a mall guide. The frantic woman was headed into another store when Sloane grabbed her arm. The woman tried to pull her arm away when Sloane spoke.

"Is that what you're looking for?" Sloane pointed.

"Oh my god! Brian! Over here Brian!" the woman rushed to him and scooped the smiling boy up.

Sloane veered away and planted herself back on the hard bench.

"Now that wasn't so bad, was it?" Aggie bumped Sloane's shoulder with her own.

"Why do I pick up so easily on kids, Aggie? The mother was closer, but I never heard her, just him."

"The easiest way to explain it is frequencies. Consider young children to have one frequency, teens another and then adults. Oh, and animals are on their own, too. Sometimes I wonder if that's the reason they don't communicate well between them all."

"Huh," was all Sloane could muster.

"Now. Do it again but push out your mind. Extend it if you will. *Expand* the frequencies."

Sloane gave the smiling Aggie a hard look and then started knocking down the walls once more.

~~*~~

It was months before Sloane stopped thinking of him a hundred times a day. It also took about that long for Aggie to start getting through her apparently dense and uncooperative mind. Within a few days of finishing the detox program the hues were more vivid than ever.

They had gone from simply glowing around a person's head to a brilliant illumination around the entire body. That had taken some getting used to, but it was the thoughts and visuals that shook her.

Sloane sat on the couch in the Den taking a break after working with Aggie all day. The constant focus on one thought only was draining for both of them. Aggie had gone out, leaving Sloane alone with her own thoughts. She hadn't gone back to her bus-driving job since the Guardianship was now paying her to be trained. Once she mastered control over the thoughts, they would let her help on missions. It was exciting and scary at the same time. Sloane was confident that if the Guardianship hadn't found her, she would not have survived much longer by herself.

Her heart clenched tight in her chest before she realized that once again, she was thinking of Liam. She wondered if she would get to work with him again. See him again. She hadn't heard a peep from him or the other Guardians except for Keagan who kept an eye on the Den and topped off the food supply. Aggie said that was normal. When on mission, the Guardians went into stealth mode and showed up when the mission was complete.

She thought about the time at the diner when she had glimpsed the cheating man's thoughts. Now she was inundated with them. Aggie had assumed she would have to teach Sloane how to read and understand people. Sloane laughed aloud. Whether teaching her how to pick out just one voice or listen when they were all blaring in her head, it wasn't going as well as Aggie hoped. At least, that's what it felt like to Sloane. It was difficult and Sloane didn't totally understand the nuances of it. Aggie hadn't been able to explain the strange power play Sloane had experienced at the institute either.

Frustration kept Sloane at the Den as much as possible when she wasn't working with Aggie. The only hues and thoughts she had to deal with here were Verity's and that was easy enough. Verity was head over heels bright yellow. Sloane smiled. She didn't think it was reciprocated but it was sweet.

Sloane thought of Liam again and wondered what he was doing just then, if he ever thought about her. She missed their playful banter, his gentle touch on her arm when he was getting her attention, and the intensity and depth behind those vibrant, blue eyes.

It was probably better this way. The emotions and sensations around him were overwhelming and intoxicating. She couldn't think straight around him.

Sloane jumped in her seat when Nia entered her peripheral. She came from nowhere and sat down at the other end of the couch. She wore designer workout clothes in black, white and pink. Sloane looked at her friend as though she was seeing her for the first time. Now that the dust had settled, and her mind was clear, she wanted answers. Nia played with the charm on her choker before bringing her pearly eyes to meet Sloane's. She finally spoke.

"At first I was your friend because I knew what you were. I knew how valuable you are. I felt the...need, don't ask me why, to protect you."

Nia stopped, blinking at the ceiling. It struck Sloane that she had always thought Nia's silver eyes were otherworldly. She just hadn't realized she was right. After pulling herself together, Nia continued.

"And then, I fell in love with you. Not in the stupid connotations that *humans* have. In truth. When you just love someone, who they are. My people give love freely and often." A silver tear rolled down her check. Sloane's eyes widened. Nia laughed, the musical sound lifting Sloane's spirits.

"What are you?" Sloane whispered.

Nia stood and removed her lightweight pink hoodie, dropping it on the couch. Her pale skin glowed bright around a black tank-top. Sloane leaned back and tilted her head. Gracefully raising her hands, palm up in a flourish, Nia drew her chin up slowly to face the ceiling. As she took in a deep breath, delicate, airy wings uncurled behind her reaching slightly further than Nia's outstretched arms. Sloane could only stare. Nia bowed, the silk veined wings following her movements.

"I'm a mountain nymph."

Sloane blinked. "Wow," she said softly. Nia rolled her eyes and reached to the couch for her hoodie. As she did, the wings curled back up and vanished from sight. Nia flopped back on the couch.

"And here I thought it would be a cold day in hell when you were speechless," Nia said. Sloane snickered.

"Why does everyone around here have wings?"

"Ah, but you're not a mere mortal my friend. You are an Aspicio, a rare and sought after breed, not just by the Guardians, but many...species."

Sloane's eyebrows shot up. "That's a scary thought." She brought her hand to her forehead and massaged it in slow circles. She sighed.

"I'll never get to have normal, will I, Nia?"

"No, honey," Nia stated softly, "but there are many of us who care about you. You're not alone in your adventure and you're not alone being different. Seen any other mountain nymphs floating around here lately?" Nia's tone had turned bitter. Sloane shook her head.

"That's because I'm the only one," Nia whispered. Sloane pressed her lips together and tilted her head as she took in Nia's sad eyes.

"I was banished from my home in Colorado. But that's a story for another time. You have guests coming and I will take my leave now." Nia stood and smiled sadly. "I do love you, my dearest friend. We'll talk again soon."

When Sloane jumped up to stop Nia, she heard a key snicking into the front door. She glanced at the door as Andy came through lugging a bag. She turned to ask Nia to stay but she was gone.

Chapter 62

Sloane sighed as Andy walked into the room, tossing the bag on the table as he went. Calm oozed from him. He had learned to keep it on constantly by Keanan, who was, she had guessed correctly when meeting him, Keppin's brother. She thought of Keanan as a Den Mother, or Father, in this case. He was married, had a baby girl and had retired from active service the year prior, but he still dropped in and kept an eye on things.

"Poker?" Andy asked as he waved a box of cards and a bag of candy in front of her.

"Sure," she said with a smile and headed to the table, "game number two thousand three hundred and five."

Andy chuckled and started to shuffle. Brick had offered to sponsor Andy, kind of like a foster parent. The Guardianship apparently had some deep hands in the pockets of various government departments. They were waiting for the appropriate paperwork to get Andy legal, but the police search for him had miraculously vanished, which was a blessing. He hadn't been able to do much without having to sneak around, though he had become pretty darn good at it. Sloane smiled.

Andy would make a wonderful Guardian.

Sloane looked at her cards and grimaced.

"Poker face," Andy reminded her. Sloane tried to straighten her face. The front door opened and Keanan walked in with a wave.

"How's everyone doing?" he asked, the usual smile on his face.

"Good," Sloane replied with a smile of her own. She wondered if Keanan and Keppin's parents were as smiley and decided she wanted to meet them.

"I have someone here I thought you might like to meet. Is Verity here by chance?"

"Nah, she went to the movies with Noah," she glanced at the clock, "They should be back anytime now."

"Oh, good. She will definitely want to see Henry. I brought some Chinese food for everyone too."

"Awesome!" Andy cheered and stood up to take the food bags. Sloane got up to meet the mystery guest who hovered behind Keanan, just out of sight.

Andy moved toward the kitchen as Keanan and his guest came further into the room. Vague recognition crossed her mind but she couldn't quite place him.

"Sloane, this is Henry. Henry, Sloane," Keanan said, making the introductions. Sloane reached out a hand and the older man clasped both of his around it.

"Wonderful to meet you at last, my dear," he said, his strong voice contradicting his age.

"At last?" Sloane dropped her hand to her side and cocked her head. The old man smiled.

"I was one of the lucky ones who was rescued from the institution. I'm also your uncle, Sloane."

"What?" Sloane said softly, her hand flying to her chest. "I have an uncle? My dad had a brother?"

"Maybe you two should have a seat?" Keanan waved to the couches. "I'll get the food set out."

Sloane sat at one end of a couch and Henry sat on the couch across from her. She was quivering from head to toe. The streak of anger over her father's desertion was replaced by surprise and curiosity.

"I was chatting with a friend just after the rescue and found out who you were. You see I was trapped there too," Henry said. "I had a few things to take care of after being there for so long, but I came here to meet you as soon as I could and bring you the truth."

Sloane watched his hue with interest as he spoke. He was feeling happy yet remorseful. She nodded at him to continue, her mouth too dry to speak.

"I bring you good and bad news," he said. Sloane felt her face involuntarily contract as tears wet her eyes.

"Your dad didn't leave you, Sloane. He never would have done that. He understood you, loved you."

"What happened?" Sloane croaked, her fears bubbling up and into her words.

"We were captured. Your father was," Henry

273

paused and closed his eyes briefly. "He was a bit more resistive than I. They drugged him into submission, only someone screwed up and he was overdosed. He didn't make it despite their efforts to keep him alive."

Sloane curled into the couch and cried. He'd been taken. He'd never meant to leave them. Out of tears, she took a deep breath and looked at Henry. Tears glistened his cheeks.

"I wish it had been me, Sloane," he said, "If I could have changed it, I want you to know I would have in a heartbeat." He coughed to stop further tears.

Sloane could only nod until her heart settled and her breath came easily once more. Someone had stolen him from her. From her mother.

"Who did this?" she asked quietly, the softness of her voice contradicted her vehemence.

"I am so sorry to tell you," he answered, "but you need to know. It was Reagan Johnson."

Chapter 63

Liam could smell the Raks' putrid scent even before he reached the small mansion.

As soon as the mission in Clearwater was complete, Liam had been called to another mission, and another eventually ending up in Montana with Kam, Ryan and Brick, to remedy a Rak threat.

Raks were the height of an average man, stooped, with thick black fur. Liam thought their faces looked like a cross between a wild cat and a pig. The foul creature's revered pain, both the delivery of it and the receipt. A Rak considered both the ultimate in sensation. Luckily there were not many clans left. They *usually* kept their torture and mayhem to animals in deeply forested, under-humanized areas.

Sloane had once asked Liam why they were called Raks. He had known right away that someone had shared some stories with her and for once he hadn't minded. He had explained to her that when they were first encountered, hundreds of years prior, their high-pitched tongue sounded like varying versions of 'rak'. No one ever seemed to be able to stay alive long enough to learn their language and find out what they called themselves, so Rak stuck.

As Liam approached the house, already shifted into his gargoyle form, he pushed thoughts of Sloane away. He needed to be focused and not get himself killed before he got to see her again.

The home was nestled at the bottom of a small mountain in the middle of Montana's lush forest. Built to blend in with the environment and be a retreat for some sought after celebrity Liam had never heard of, the Raks must have stumbled upon it and wreaked their havoc.

Kam's shadowed figure hovered to the right of the back door in the darkness. Ryan's appeared to the left only a moment later. Liam looked at Brick and waited for the signal. A quick nod and all four of them drew long, razor sharp swords. With humans you didn't need weapons. With Raks, the more the better. Liam had already triple checked the knives stashed in his belts and the straps across his chest and legs.

The smell was so strong he wondered if the Raks had tunneled into the house as per usual or used the back door. Brick opened the screen door and turned the doorknob. He easily broke the lock and swung the door open, sword held out in front and downward. Liam moved in directly behind him, sword in one hand, and a long bowie knife in the other.

They entered a large kitchen and spread out immediately, Liam and Brick on either side of a hallway that according to the blueprints led to the remainder of the house. Kam shadowed

Liam, constantly glancing behind and Ryan did the same for Brick.

They glided through the silent house checking the rooms as they went, looking for any obvious signs of the Raks. The house was decked out in wood, gray tones and all the colors of metal. They found a large double door entry in the back of the far side of the house.

Brick grabbed the right handle. Liam went to his left with Kam behind him and Ryan flanked Brick's right. Brick pulled open the door and Liam slipped in and to the right. Brick followed on his heels and went left. Ryan and Kam fell in behind them.

It was a huge ballroom built straight into the mountain. Half of the room was decorated in Victorian decor. Gold and burgundy lit up the walls with color, stone pillars topped with antique vases stood next to floor-to-ceiling columns. The other half of the room was dug straight into the dark mountain stone. Tapestries from a time long forgotten covered part of the walls. Three crude holes gaped in the stone, dark tunnels disappearing downward. Liam moved in between the two holes on the right, Kam in between the two on the left, leaving Brick and Ryan to take the outside

Swords ready, Brick had only just given the signal to enter when Raks poured out from the chasms, chomping out the high-pitched screams that got them their name. Clutching primitive axes and clubs, they attacked.

"Ambush!" Kam growled. The Guardians

moved without hesitation.

Brick brought his sword down and over cutting in to three Raks at one time. Kam stabbed one in the gut with a dagger and swung his sword across the throat of another bringing them both down with deadly efficiency. Ryan swung his cudgel, crushing head after head into a bloody mess. Liam wielded his sword and knife like a ballet, slicing off arms, hands and heads as they rushed toward him. In minutes the floor was slick with the dark oily blood of Raks.

And they kept coming.

The relentless swarm of Raks into the room forced the Guardians away from the ragged tunnels. There was no time to coordinate, only to act.

Kam's growl brought up Liam's head. Liam had only a fraction of a second to watch Kam's left arm drop to his side, a fillet hanging from his bicep. Liam immediately started to fight his way over to Kam but the sheer numbers rushing him prevented any progress. With a hard swing of his sword, he cleaved another club wielding arm from its owner. He spared a glance to Kam and was relieved to see him still holding his own despite having only one sword arm, his wings had become his second weapon.

Liam turned and sliced, lunged and stabbed, digging his claws into the ground so he wouldn't slip. Brick needed a moment to breath to bring out the tornado, but they wouldn't let up. They were putting less attention on Kam, maybe due to his injury. Ryan was moving so fast, he was blurring and yet Raks were on him four deep. Liam started his way toward Ryan, hacking through the small but muscled Raks, leaving a pile of bodies behind him.

He was only two yards away when Ryan went down. He didn't make a sound, but Brick did. His roar echoed through the room. He was surrounded. Throwing out his sword arms Brick changed, the whorls of gray taking him over yet leaving his outstretched hands free of the deadly spin. Knocking bodies helter-skelter, he moved toward Ryan and Liam. Blood sprayed periodically from the gray cloud and Liam knew Brick had been hit.

Ryan was hit? And then Brick? Their skin was virtually indestructible and yet, Liam was racing to save them. It made no sense.

He moved faster than ever and still they came. A jarring pain struck his shoulder and he faltered. He fell to one knee as he turned to fillet his attacker. The Raks head slid downward and Liam quickly dispatched the next two in line.

The scream of spinning air and the war cries of Raks being tossed like rag dolls were somehow comforting. Liam spun and sliced, a spray of thick blood hitting his face. Before he could wipe his eyes, unfathomable pain seared down his backside, ripping out a strangled cry.

As he plummeted to the ground, he thought of Sloane.

Lisa Barry

Chapter 64

Andy laid down his Ace with smile. Sloane's mouth dropped. "You so cheated," she accused, her lips curling up. Andy laughed as he pulled the hard candies they were using as chips toward his growing pile.

Sloane got up. "Your deal. This time, you're going *down*. But first, I need some water."

"In your dreams," Andy taunted and started shuffling. Sloane headed toward the kitchen.

Halfway there, an odd noise came from her, a soft intake of breath. Andy looked up to see her drop heavily to her knees. She hissed in pain and hugged herself. Andy jumped up and ran as she crumbled to the floor.

"Help!" Andy hollered as he skidded to a stop in front of her. He put his hands on her shoulder, no idea what to do. Aggie rushed in and knelt beside him. Moving his hands away, she felt Sloane's neck. Aggie's face gave no indication of what was happening. She backed away from Sloane.

"Go ahead and pick her up, bring her to her room," she told him. Andy looked at Sloane and then back at Aggie. "It's alright, boy. Get her into her bed."

Andy nodded and ever so gently picked Sloane up. She whimpered and he fought not to show his fear. Aggie went ahead of him and pulled back the comforter and sheets. He laid Sloane down carefully then stood aside to watch her. She curled away from him onto her side and pulled her arms and legs close. Tears dribbled from her closed eyes and her lips pressed firmly together.

Aggie tucked a stray hair away from Sloane's face. "Sloane, can you hear me?" she asked.

Sloane's back stiffened and then her whole body trembled in reply. Andy watched her fight something they couldn't see and fought off tears of his own. Sloane stiffened again, a low whine piercing the silent room. Andy wondered...he reached out for the hem of her shirt.

"What..." Aggie started and Andy waved a hand at her. He pulled Sloane's shirt up. His eyes widened, and he slowly went to his knees as he stared.

Aggie rushed around the bed and stopped. A bloodless, jagged wound was cleaved to bone from Sloane's shoulder down to her hip.

Chapter 65

Hours later Sloane came to and she knew. The searing pain she had felt was now a dull throb, fading faster by the minute. She curled up as tight as possible on her bed and sobbed quietly in the darkness. It was his bed really. *Was?* She had kept his pillow after he'd left and she buried into it now wishing and hoping she was wrong.

Chapter 66

Within hours of her strange incident, the cut on her back had vanished as though it had never been there. Within days, life was back to normal with the exception of the added visits and phone calls with her Uncle Henry.

Three weeks later Brick showed up with Keppin to collect Andy for school. Though she hadn't seen Keppin for weeks, she stayed in her room, heart numb. She could hear them. Andy and Keppin gleefully discussing the training they would finally get from the Guardianship's school, located in Europe no less. Brick's deep baritone and Aggie's gruff voice were also exchanging words, but they didn't quite penetrate her closed door.

Anger and loss filled Sloane's head. She threw open her door and stood before them all, arms wrapped around her chest. She stared at Brick's back, questions filling her eyes. Brick turned and met her eyes. The sadness was deep. He pursed his lips and shook his head. Aggie started toward her, concern etched into her weary face. Sloane's lip quivered before she turned back to her room, grabbed her purse and left the condo without a word.

Chapter 67

Giggling as she held on to the rustic wooden bar, Sloane tried to keep from sliding off her stool. The man next to her smiled. He was handsome, if a fair bit older than her, and she had taken a brotherly love to him immediately. He reminded her of someone, not that she could remember who. After several drinks it was not surprising that his hue had gone from a pleasant light yellow to the typical green and purple hue men seemed to gravitate toward under any and all circumstances.

Actually, she had no idea what he'd just said. Between the alcohol, concentrating on not tipping off the stool and all the colors and thoughts floating around, she kept getting distracted. She had come here to...she scrunched her face for a moment. She couldn't quite remember.

The man made a motion toward the door and Sloane suddenly felt tired. She took her blue jean, black tee clad self and slipped off the stool. Her legs didn't seem to be working and the floor slid closer.

Her brother caught her just before she landed in a heap and she giggled at her good fortune.

Then she remembered. She didn't even have a brother. She giggled again. Somehow, the man helped her out the door. The salty air filled her lungs, suddenly making her want to take a walk on the beach.

The man was talking, she could tell that words were coming out of his mouth but none of them made any sense. A bat flew overhead, and she could understand it's images better than the man. She laughed again. They were walking slowly, the man holding her up with an arm. Sloane's hand was a vice grip on his shoulder in an attempt to stay upright. He motioned with a free hand to a car parked curbside just two spots away and they shuffled forward.

Liam perched on a flat roof in gargoyle form. He concentrated on the door to the bar. She was in there. He could feel her presence almost as clearly as the familiar hum of adrenalin pumping through his veins.

Logic told him to leave, told him to let her live life without him, without this new burden he carried. But the string that bound them together whispered something else. It murmured softly and seductively, a cruel chant in his mind that he couldn't seem to tuck away.

She exited the bar hanging sloppily on a man's arm. And laughing.

The sight blocked logic like a fallen rock and his muscles tensed for battle. He watched, waiting as they neared the shadow of the building. Roiling his skin, he prepared to move.

Shadows crept over them and he jumped, throwing out his wings and sweeping in from behind.

Sloane was lifted from the man's arm and her face shoved into his chest to quiet her startled scream. Liam cold-cocked the man before he even registered Sloane was gone. Catching him as he fell, Liam eased the body down to rest against the wall. Just another drunk who didn't make it to his car.

Seconds later they were airborne. Heading north from the beach, they were over the gulf water when Sloane's body began convulsing in his arms. Searching below, he found a small island thankfully void of partying teenagers. Landing near a tree, he gently held Sloane's body out and pulled her hair back just in time contents of her stomach to empty onto the sand. Amaretto sours. When she had settled down, limp in his arms, they took to the air once more.

Waking up in a foreign bed, sheets tucked around her, was more than disturbing. The room was dark and her head was pounding. Sloane tried to remember how many drinks she'd had and gave up. She couldn't even remember leaving the bar. This was b.a.d. bad. She lifted a hand to rub her forehead when a sound made her stop short.

She strained to hear, the silence a loud buzz in her head. And then she heard it again. A soft sigh. A familiar tone. Her chest clenched. Peering into the darkness, she could vaguely make out a side table and beyond it a wall. She slowly turned over.

She slammed her eyes closed in shock and then in embarrassment. Her chest pounded in surprise and joy, unsure if she should be thrilled or scared. Even in the dark his beautiful features were unmistakable.

"You can chill, I know you're awake," his deep rumble startled her. Sloane so wanted to say something witty but the pounding in her head prevented it from arriving. She didn't say anything for a long time. Being in bed with Liam was something she had envisioned many times, but these circumstances fit her visions about as well as a horse through a mouse hole. Especially once she realized her breath would likely kill a small child. She turned back over and finally spoke to the wall.

"I thought you were dead," she whispered.

"I'm not," he answered, his voice void of any emotion.

"Why am I here?" she asked as anger sparked at his cold reply.

"It looked to me like you needed help." His voice was mostly calm, just a hint of annoyance. She felt him roll out of the bed.

"Am I kidnapped? Are you stalking me?" she asked sarcastically.

"No. I don't need to stalk you. I just know

how to find you."

Sloane turned over again to glare at his silhouette. He was sitting in a chair at the foot of the bed. Lest he keel over, she covered her mouth before saying anything. "Why am I here?"

Liam's frustrated sigh stoked the anger building in her chest.

"Your *step-father*," he said like he was talking about a repulsive psycho maniac, which he actually was, "is running around free and needs to be removed."

"Removed? Not that I disagree but removing *humans* is not exactly in The Guardian's play book." The headache didn't seem quite as bad. Sloane wondered if irritation helped. Doubtful.

"No, it's not. I asked." This time his sigh sounded beaten. She tried to keep her anger, but it abated like an untied balloon.

"Trust me, not that I don't completely agree with you, but what can I do about it?"

"I need you to tell me everything you know about him, anything and everything you can think of."

"What good is that if you can't do anything about it?"

"Sloane," he drew her name out in a soft hum and ran a hand through his hair. Was that nervousness? Sloane sent out a tendril of power. She just barely felt the frustration rolling off him. That was new. She pulled up onto an elbow, frowning.

"What is going on?"

What little emotion she'd felt from him

vanished. The shadows of the room kept her from reading his face. He slumped down in the chair and spoke, his voice so soft she almost missed it.

"I've gone rogue."

A Note from Lisa

I hope that you enjoyed reading this book as much as I enjoyed writing it. If you did, I would love it if you could take a few minutes to help others find and enjoy it by leaving a review or sharing with a friend!

If you would like to find out how the first Guardian came to be, please join my mailing list to receive the free short story *Origins*. Origins is very near and dear to my heart as it was the starting point, the first idea that made my heart jump and prompted me to sit down and write this series.

If you pop over to my website (authorlisabarry.com) and click on the Newsletter link you'll receive the free short story plus information on new releases and other random stuff!

Rogue, Book Two in the Gargoyles Den series is available at several retailers.

Found, Book Three, the final in the series is scheduled near the end of 2019.

Lisa Barry

About Me

From the age of five, I grew up in Florida which I quickly found was not a good enough reason to avoid wearing black. A daily color choice, I constantly pine for weather cool enough to wear boots but I generally just stay locked indoors. :)

I live with my incredibly supportive (and hot) husband and amazingly awesome kidlets. I count it a blessing that they still love me despite the deafening sound of my music muse throughout the house.

Writing and reading every minute I can, I count on the many gargoyles who listen carefully when I read to them aloud. As you might have guessed, I collect gargoyles and books. I also LOVE to travel (always planning my next trip to Ireland!) and enjoy time with friends and family.

I love hearing from my readers, feel free to reach out!

Email: authorlisabarry@gmail.com

facebook.com/authorlisabarry

twitter.com/authorlisabarry

THE GUARDIANS

Also by Lisa

The Gargoyles Den series

Origins
The Guardians
Rogue
Found

<u>Ruby Dust</u>, a stand-alone short story

Ghirn, sheriff of Ruby Dust on Mars, catches an outlaw, saves a couple of humans from cannibalistic Dearndins and calms the ladies of The Pink House. All in a day's work.

Short stories - available in these Ink Slingers Guild anthologies:

The Lottery, <u>Beyond the Cosmos</u>
Happily Ever After, <u>Veiled Affection</u>
Hearts of Monsters, <u>Serenity Rising</u>
Kitten's Play, <u>On the Verge</u>
Tommi's Relocations, LLC, <u>Behind the Veil</u>
Who is the Predator? <u>Super Useless</u>
Beginnings, <u>Into the Abyss</u>
The Spellmart Incident, <u>The Death of Jimmy</u>
Closure, <u>The Purge of Jimmy</u>

Protect your Mental Health Rights

Unscientific Mental Health Diagnoses

One of the fundamental flaws of psychiatry is its unscientific diagnostic system. Unlike proper medical diagnosis, psychiatry categorize symptoms only, not disease. The American Psychiatric Association's Diagnostic and Statistical Manual is notorious for its low scientific validity. In it, even "spending much more money than intended" is listed as a symptom of a mental illness— for which psychotropic medication is often prescribed.

Harmful Psychotropic Drugs

Drugging with psychotropic medication is a preferred treatment of psychiatry. These drugs are synthetic chemicals that pass the blood-brain barrier and can cause serious side effects. Here are but a few of the warnings for one of the most commonly prescribed anti-depressant drug:

• Hypertension
• Increased weight
• Varicose veins
• Amnesia
• Hallucination
• Suicidal tendency

And even though the drug is classified as an "anti-depressant", one of its FDA listed side effects is— depression.

THE GUARDIANS

There ARE other Solutions

Many Non-Profit organizations and individuals are concerned about the excesses and harmful practices of psychiatry. The Citizens Commission on Human Rights (CCHR) of Florida is a non-profit organization that investigates and exposes psychiatric violations of human rights. CCHR Florida also educates Americans about their mental health rights, including the right to informed consent.

CCHR Florida works side-by-side with like-minded groups and individuals who share a common purpose to stop abuses in the field of mental health. Together, they have formed a strong movement that is especially active to help protect the rights of children. We invite you to join our efforts to bring compassion and decency to the field of mental health.

The Right to Say "NO"

A fundamental human right is the right to be fully informed of the possible consequences of a medication or treatment. Part of this right is the right to say no to a drug that you don't want to take or that you don't want your child to take. Call or email CCHR Florida if you want to know more or need help. 800-782-2878; info@cchrflorida.org